TO DIE IN CLONMEL

TO DIE IN CLONMEL

JOHN O'DWYER

First published 2024 by John O'Dwyer
Dublin, Ireland

First edition

British Library Cataloguing in Publication Data.
A catalogue record for this book is available from the National Library of Ireland and the
British Library.

Typesetting and design by Carrowmore.ie

ROTATION

The snot that hung from my nose was finally blown away by the biting March wind. It fell on the crossbar of the plough between my purple hands. I did my best to guide it through the stony impoverished soil as I followed Molly's ponderous arse up the hill. The heat from the horse's breath wafted back at me a reminder that somewhere there was a place where you could be warm, but with Molly, the sudden burst of hot air meant we had hit another rock.

The plough jumped out of the furrow and skidded sideways.

'Blast it, Molly!' I shouted. Molly ignored me and dropped her head to the withered grass. She was used to it now. I would take the bar that hung from the plough and lever out the stone, then I would pull the plough back to the furrow and start again.

The rock was larger than usual, but then so was I. I lifted it and stumbled across the ploughed ground to the nearest rock pile. I dropped it on top. It rolled off and I had to jump to save my toes. I got an insane desire to kick it, but good sense returned just in time. As I walked back to Molly, I looked down the valley towards the great house where once I had lived. I saw the lush green fields that flowed from it in every direction, green except for the ploughed field where I noted with envy the beauty of the straight furrows. I had met the ploughman for the big house the previous day going into Mass. Ned Butler was his name, and he was walking in front of me. I was hanging back, but he stopped walking as he gazed up the hill towards my ploughing and I caught up, hoping to slip by, but no such luck.

'John' he said to me, 'you will have to give up the poteen.' And added, after further study, 'Sure Molly must be on it as well.'

I looked at him stung. He waited for me to say something, his craggy face looking up at me, back bent, the hand on his blackthorn stick supporting his weight, knobby with arthritis. I was about to say that at least I am straight. Then a little voice in my head said that is what I will look like at his age.

'What age are you?' I asked. It took him by surprise.

'Forty-five,' he answered. Then I felt sorry for us both, and at the end of the day, his furrows were straight, and mine were crooked. Then we both went into Mass. He stayed at the back and I went up the church to join James in the second pew. James was my stepbrother, the son of my father's wife, a delicate gentlewoman who passed away after giving birth. I sat beside him. Everyone said he was like his mother – small and frail. But I knew better. He was dressed as and behaved like a rich landowner; but a rich landowner he no longer was. We lived in a hovel on the side of a hill.

It was James's idea to plough a field that was never turned before. I leaned over and whispered in his ear, 'Rotation. You and your fecking rotation.'

PERFECT
CHRISTIANS

The priest appeared on the altar, flanked by two altar boys. Fr Watkins was his name, a florid-faced man with a paunch. I had once been an altar boy, but left in disgrace having sampled a bottle of wine foolishly left open an unattended in the sacristy. I would have gotten away with it but for the hiccups which led to stomach upheaval which led to wine squirting in every direction as I tried to stop it with my hand. Fr Watkins looked nervously at the front seat for a moment. I didn't know why as there was nobody there. Lord Stapleton, who now owned the big house (thus ensuring his right to sit in the front seat) had travelled to England the previous week. I, for one, was glad he was not there, as he made no effort to conceal his distaste at our sitting so close to him. The priest was one of those who liked to hear a word echo before saying another. He started to give his sermon. This was when I sat sideways in my seat, trying to get as many women in my view as possible. I struggled to identify which ones were doing all the fornication and immodest touching that Fr Watkins was always talking about. The touching was not happening in church, that's for sure, as the women were not allowed to sit on the same side as the men. It was hard to get so much as a bad thought, as all could be seen of a woman was a nose protruding from a scarf. Through the mist of my indifference to the drone of the priest's voice came strange words which snapped my attention back to the sermon. I struggled to understand his words. Instead of telling us we were all sinners and doomed to eternal hellfire if we did not change our ways, he was telling us we were devout Christians. We should be proud of it, and we were surely bound for heaven if we remained so.

He finished by saying he had been promoted, and would be leaving us to accept this great honour. In his absence, Fr O'Brien and Fr Tobin, on their way to their new parish, would say Mass for us. Paddy was next up. Paddy took the collection, and it was his job to read the names of the people who donated and the amounts contributed. The collection was the most interesting part of the Mass for us, as the holy part was conducted in Latin. We dozed through it, but nobody slept through the reading of the collection.

Paddy was good at it, and he paused for dramatic effect after each name before announcing the amount given, while we compared in our minds the donations with the status of the donor. We watched as those who considered themselves superior were shocked that some upstart had given more. That meant next month's donation would have to be increased to confirm their ranking in the parish. James name was called, and established his standing as number two in the congregation with a generous offering. I wondered where he got it.

'Finally,' said Paddy, with a flourish turning the page, 'Lord Stapleton.'

At this stage, he would genuflect in the direction of the front pew and read the amount. But confusion reigned. There was nothing on the page. Paddy turned towards the priest for an explanation but he was gone. After Mass, we gathered in groups to discuss everything that happened during the week, and quickly dismissed the lack of a donation from 'Lordy', as we called him, as an oversight for which some of his staff would pay dearly. We went on to talk about who died and who got married. The best stories were about who Fr Watkins chased out of Finnigan's hay-barn after the dance at the crossroads. This was undoubtedly where the priest got the material for his sermons on fornication, although it was usually the same woman each time. This was enough to condemn the rest of us as fornicators when we had no such luck.

A FOOL AND
HIS PANTS

The ploughing being finished, James and I were loading the piles of stones on a cart, with Molly standing patiently between the shafts. Molly saw them first, her head rising, ears pricked. I followed her gaze. The three elders of the parish were picking their way through the furrows.

'Here comes trouble,' I said to James.

'Faith, Hope and Charity,' James guessed without turning.

'Yes,' I confirmed.

That's what James called them. They came to James when they had a problem with Lordy. They seemed to think that because we once lived in the big house that Lordy would listen to us; plus, once, after Lordy had taken over, they had approached him about some piddling matter and he threw them out.

They did not like being humiliated, so they came to James to plead their case. That Lordy would humble us did not matter to them. James would go; he always did.

Faith spoke first. Religion, I thought. James had explained the nicknames. Faith spoke on theology and church, Hope on rent and Charity on hardship.

'He locked them up,' Faith blurted.

James carefully placed the stone he was carrying on the cart before turning.

'Who locked who up?' James asked.

'The priests. Fr Tobin and Fr O'Brien,' Faith blurted. 'Lord Stapleton locked them up.'

I had never seen Faith so excited. His small body trembled, moustache bristling with anger.

'Why?' asked James.

'No one knows,' said Hope.

'That is what we would like you to find out,' said Charity.

'I will ask him,' replied James.

'When? There is a crowd gathering. There could be trouble,' Faith added.

'Now.'

James began to walk.

'We will go now,' he said to me.

'Like this?' I asked, holding out my arms to display my woollen jumper with numerous holes through which could be seen a shirt whose original colour could only be guessed at. Pants belonging to my father when times were good, only held in place by a sturdy leather belt, also my father's.

'We look fine,' said James, because he always did.

There was an angry crowd milling at the walls when we got there, barred from entering by the closed gates and a line of soldiers we had never seen before. They looked like they would not mind a bit of trouble. James pushed his way through the crowd, telling them quietly to move back.

'James Landers to see Lord Stapleton.'

This to the soldier plainly in charge.

'He might not want to see you,' the soldier replied, locking eyes with James.

'Then again he might, do you want to take that chance?'

The soldier's eyes wavered.

'Follow me,' he ordered. The gate opened and we entered the courtyard.

The great house was built in uncertain times. Stables enclosed the cobbled area we stood in on one side, with living quarters facing us on the other. The house itself ensured a secure twenty foot barrier between those inside and any would-be intruders.

'Wait here,' was the curt command.

Across the cobbled yard, three soldiers were playing a game with much excitement on the stone sundial which dominated its centre. James had fallen silent as he studied the house where a generation of our family had once lived, a faraway look in his eyes.

'Which one?' I heard a soldier ask.

Driven by curiosity, I moved closer to observe. I saw three shells on the stone. The soldier lifted one of them. There was a pea underneath.

'Watch closely,' he advised, as he pushed the shells.

I did just that. Now and then he would raise a shell and show the pea. Then he finished.

'I bet a coin you can't find the pea!' he challenged his growing audience.

I had watched and knew where the pea was.

'That one.'

A soldier who had been watching from the very beginning lifted the shell, and there it was just as I had thought.

'You win again!' the one with the shells said, handing the other soldier a coin. The pea was inserted and shuffled.

'Which one? he asked this time. He asked me.

'Just a game,' he said, 'to test your skill.'

I lifted the shell and sure enough, there was the pea. It was easy.

'I bet you a coin you can't do that again,' he said, visibly impressed.

'I could,' I said, 'but I don't have a coin.'

'That will do nicely,' he said, pointing to my leather belt with the brass buckle that was my pride and joy. As I hesitated, he moved the shells and I saw the pea. It was under the one on the right.

'You have a bet! I said triumphantly, raising the shell.

There was no pea. I gave him the belt and had to put my hand in my pocket to hold up my pants.

How had I got it wrong?

'Give me another chance,' I pleaded, flushed with dismay at losing my one and only family heirloom. He looked me up and down from my woolly jumper with the holes, dirty shirt, baggy pants and worn, scuffed boots and said, with genuine sadness, 'you have nothing else I want.'

I was about to appeal to James, who was now looking on for a coin, when the officer came back and said, 'His Lordship will see you now.'

We walked towards the front door of the great house only to be confronted by the officer.

'Not that way – through the servants' quarters.'

We made our way through the kitchen where maids with red, sweaty faces were piling food on plates. We followed them up the stairs to the dining room where a dozen lords and their ladies were dining. It quickly became apparent they were only dressed as such, as serving maids dodged the lords' groping hands while the ladies whooped with laughter.

Lordy sat at the head of the table, looking bored by it all. We stood there waiting. I could see the colour rising on James's neck as it became plain we were being ignored. That – and my rumbling stomach – prompted me to shout over the din.

'Could we have some food while we wait for his Lordship to finish his meal?'

That got his attention. He would have to talk to us, feed us, or throw us out. Lordy stood up, banging a goblet of the table for attention; there was silence.

'Look,' he said, 'look at what remains of a family of chieftains who once ruled these lands and sat where I sit. See this chieftain and his warrior, reduced to common serfs.'

He paused, his voice dripping with contempt.

'What are you begging for now?' he finished.

I took my hands out of my pockets, my temper rising as my pants descended with equal speed. Whoops of laughter rang around the hall. Even Lordy joined in. The mood had changed.

'What do you want this time?' asked Lordy.

'I want you to free the priests,' said James.

Lordy went to the window and looked out.

'Is that your army out there?' he asked, looking at the gathering crowd outside the walls.

Walking out, so the crowd could see him, he held up his arms for quietness and proclaimed, 'If ye come back tomorrow at noon, the priests will be freed in the company of your great leader. James.'

We left through the kitchen again. I spoke with Martha, the cook, who slipped me a lump of meat and told me how she missed the old days. The soldier with the shells was still there at the sundial. One of the maids from the kitchen had brought him food, and whatever she had lost to him caused her to go bright red. I noticed this as she passed me, as I pleaded with James for a coin to win back my belt. To my surprise, he agreed and approached the soldier.

'I have no coin,' he said, 'just this.' And he took from his finger a ring that was his mother's and her mother's before her. Now I did not want him to play, and assured him that a bit of rope would hold up my pants just fine. James ignored me.

'Five coins and the belt against the ring.'

The soldier's eyes lit up, placing five coins and the belt on the sundial beside the ring. The soldier moved the shells, showing the pea now and then. The three shells came to a stop. I had followed every move of the pea and knew which one it was under. James put his hand on another. I tried to

16

tell him he was wrong. He lifted the shell, and there was the pea to the astonishment of both the soldier and myself. James scooped the shells into his hand and handed them to the soldier who was speechless with shock.

Before he could recover, James handed him his coins back and said, 'I would like to talk to the priests.'

Glad of his money back, he led James to a barred window and went back to the sundial to play his game. I watched, but this time my belt stayed on. James rejoined me deep in thought and silent as we walked home.

I waited for an explanation; none came. Finally, I broke.

'How did you know which shell?' I blurted.

'Hold out your hand,' he ordered. I did, so he put some peas in my hand and some in his mouth and began to chew.

'We passed through the kitchen,' he said. 'Plenty of peas.'

A WELL-MADE POINT

We were back at noon. This time we were not stopped at the gates. Behind us were Faith, Hope and Charity – and what appeared to be the entire population of the parish – to celebrate the freeing of their priests. The soldiers were there again. No games this time. They lined the way to the great house door which stood open. Barring our way was the surly officer we met on the first day.

'Just you two.'

We walked past him and the doors banged shut behind us. We climbed the stairs to where they sat as before, eating and drinking. Lordy was at the entrance to greet us.

'Welcome, great Irish chieftain,' he greeted James. 'I trust your warlord will not display his weapon today!'

There was a little laughter, but it was nervous.

'Please sit,' Lordy invited.

There were three empty chairs at the head of the table, at which Lordy waved a hand.

'Take your rightful place,' he said.

James walked in front of me to the head of the table and pulled back Lordy's chair. Lordy had stopped smiling.

'Sit, my lord,' said James.

Lordy took his seat, smiling again, and we took ours.

'Eat, drink,' Lordy said, beckoning the maid.

I was already in action, carving a huge slice of meat from the joint in front of me. The razor-sharp blade I left lodged in the meat for further reference. The maid filled my cup with wine. I was in heaven. I smiled at her, but she seemed tense and did not respond. Two servants came in and opened the shutters on the window facing the courtyard; there was something vaguely familiar about them, but I was too busy eating to care.

I looked at James. His hands hung by his side. He was watching Lordy, who in turn was studying him.

After some thought, Lordy asked James, 'What do you owe them, those peasants who have you coming here, begging for lower rents, more land help with the roof of their church, and now the return of their priests? Do you want to remain a beggar? Or sit once again in this chair? I was in England recently and secured a very advantageous post. I have plans beyond this valley, leaving this estate in the hands of a man who knows its problems, who hopefully will have learned from the mistakes of his father who fed those peasants outside through three bad years and turned his son into a beggar. A man who would sire a bastard son with a housemaid.'

I looked up.

'A man,' he continued, 'who could not live with his incompetence and hung himself from this chair.'

James had paled but said nothing.

'Now let me know what it is you want. Come, I will show you your choices so you can better make up your mind.'

He draped his hand around James's shoulder and they walked to the window.

'I will put you in charge of all you once owned. That or remain forever a beggar for that rabble.'

James looked down at the expectant crowd. I heard him say, 'I will discuss that with you after you free the priests.'

I sat back in my chair, thinking how well things were going.

'Ahh yes,' Lordy said, 'the priests. There were conditions to the post I secured. I undertook to show support for a new order, a new regime that did not include priests. That was my choice and I am afraid that by insisting on their freedom, you have made yours. Free the priests!' Lordy said in a loud voice that startled me.

Two large black birds appeared in the window flapping their wings, but they were not birds; they were the priests hanging by their necks from the floor above. I had not noticed the spare rope until the two servants caught James, put the rope around his neck and threw him out the window. I could hear a scream of rage and despair. It came from me as I cleared the table, snatching the knife from the meat as I passed. The servants had turned towards me, and as I crashed into them I recognised the shell player and his partner. I slashed with the knife. The shell player jumped back. My onward force caused me to crash into his partner and he fell out the window. I grabbed the twitching rope, sliding down as I hacked at it with the knife. I caught a glimpse of James holding on to the rope for dear life.

We dropped. The cobblestones flashed through my mind on the way down, but we did not hit them. We landed on Faith, Hope and Charity and the soldier who was sitting up, nursing his arm. I pulled James to his feet. I wanted to run, but James was looking up at Lordy and his guests who were crowded into the window looking down.

Lordy could have ordered his soldiers to finish us then, but he wanted to prove a point. He addressed the heads that surrounded him in the window.

'Behold James Landers, who came here in front of an army of people to make demands. James Landers, pay attention while I make a point. Yee down there,' he addressed the crowd, 'you sent those two to me as beggars and beggars they shall be. Anyone who gives them alms, I will hang and evict their family. Anyone who speaks to them, I will hang and evict their family.'

Looking down on us in a crowd who had gathered around us, he went on.

'Anyone who touches them, I will hang.'

They fell over themselves backing away, even the soldier with the injured arm.

Lordy went on, 'The property they own belongs to the first person who lays a hand on it. If they are in this valley tomorrow, fifty coins for each of their dead bodies.'

'Time to go, James,' I said, catching him by the arm. I had listened to the last offer and could see a lot of loopholes, none of them to our advantage. James had to have his say.

He drew himself up and proclaimed, 'I will sit in my father's chair again and I will judge you.'

It came out as a croak because of the damage to his throat. I hoped Lordy did not hear it, but he did. His face darkened.

'Begone from here, beggars, before I change my mind.'

I would have run but James croaked at me, 'With dignity, with dignity.'

We walked, but people ran to get out of our way first, though they followed on behind. Then some ran ahead. Then a race started. When we crossed the road to climb to our hovel, we could see up ahead the fastest making off with Molly. Mucky the sow was dragged away, protesting loudly as her bonhams dispersed in all directions. Feathers flew as the hens were rounded up. The side of bacon we had smoking up the chimney was on a man's shoulder. It was Charity. A fortunate neighbour who had brought his dog was herding the sheep away.

By the time we got there with our dignified walk, everything was gone. Something to keep us warm became our search. The blankets were gone. In the outhouse were some old corn sacks. I wondered why they were still there, until I moved them and a family of baby rats were exposed. I shook them free and put the bags under my arm and walked through the stony ploughed field that I now thought fondly of, into the woods and the unknown.

James walked beside me deep in thought, before saying as much to himself as to me, 'Lordy made his point well.'

VOCATION

The rain poured down. The sack over my shoulder became a water-filled burden so that, even between showers, the water continued to run down between the cheeks of my arse, down the trouser leg and into the rising water seeping up through the holes in my boots. I opened my mouth to say we will get no work today, and closed it again. He would know that. I opened it again to say I am hungry, and closed it again; he would know that. I was always hungry.

I opened it again to ask where we were going to sleep tonight, and closed it again; even he did not know that.

I studied his slight fiveand-a-half foot frame as he strode purposefully along, taking two steps to my one, his eyes fixed on the turn ahead like a man whose castle was around that bend. He seemed so unaffected by the rain that I stared at him for a while to see if it was hitting him at all. I stopped to relieve myself and to examine the surrounding bushes for any berries that had survived the winter. I caught up with him at the turn of the road.

He was standing looking down the valley, nostrils extended, breathing deeply. Steam was rising off the ground as the sun broke through the clouds to shine on the sodden wretches beneath, soon to disappear over the horizon, to allow the chill of the night to hurry us on our way to the wasting disease and death.

'We could join the army,' I suggested.

'Which one?' he asked absent-mindedly.

'You are the one who knows about those things,' I pointed out. 'Would they both feed you?' I asked.

He nodded.

'Boots and clothes?'

He nodded again.

'And horses?'

'Yes,' he said, 'horses too.'

I paused for thought, my brow furrowed. I remembered how the parish best had looked after a faction fight, and that was only fists and cudgels, not swords and muskets.

'Do you know which side will win?'

'Yes,' he said.

'Then we will join that side!' I concluded triumphantly.

'You would not mind hanging a few priests then?' he inquired.

The vision of celebrating a glorious victory on a white charger vanished, and was replaced by a devil using a sprong on my rear end.

Something had caught his attention. I followed his gaze a wisp of smoke. And something else. My stomach rumbled as the breeze brought the welcome smell of frying bacon.

We shambled forwards, our legs no longer controlled by our minds, just the gnawing hunger we were forced to address. A mud hut abandoned so long that a mature tree had grown through the roof, creating a hole that the smoke was using as a chimney. What we looked like I don't know. The sight of James filling the doorway, with my head resting on his shoulder to get a view, was frightening enough to cause one of them to jump up, his head hitting a rafter, causing a shower of debris to shower down on the other man who remained sitting – but thankfully missing the pan holding the frying bacon, sizzling on the remains of the fireplace.

Two priests. My heart sank, even if they were willing to share; there was only enough for me. Then I noticed a loaf of bread on a stone. All was not lost.

'God save all here,' James greeted them.

'God save you, my son,' the older one replied.

'We are hungry, Father,' James said. 'We would be grateful if you could spare some food.'

'Of course, there is plenty for everyone,' the younger priest assured us.

The older one said, 'Help yourself.'

I reached down and rescued a slice of bacon from the pan. I began to chew, relishing the burned crispy hair as much as the lean meat as much as the juicy fat. I became aware James was staring at me.

'What?' I enquired.

'Grace, Father Tobin,' he said.

I was about to say 'I will put that on the bread' when I noticed he had joined his hands and was looking up to heaven. I began to pray. My mind scrambled between trying to swallow the bacon and think why James had called me Fr Tobin.

'Fr O'Brien and Fr Tobin!' the older priest exclaimed, 'My prayers are answered.'

'Mine too,' said James, a look of relief and warning in his eyes as he turned towards me.

Priest

My mind started to follow what was happening. James had got their names from the two priests in Lordy's jail. He had been heading here all the time.

'I understand you had some trouble in the parish where we are bound?' James asked the old one.

'The parish is ruled by murderers and thieves!' the younger one blurted.

'They ran us out,' the older one admitted.

'You may fare no better where you travel,' James warned.

'Yes,' I said. 'Priests are hung on sight there.'

James added, 'We had to dress in those rags to avoid suspicion, and even then we were searched. Luckily we were warned in time to throw away our clerical cloth. Now, however, we enter our new parish dressed as tramps.'

'We could swap clothes?' the young one offered.

'Yes,' agreed the old one, 'perhaps it may be safer.'

Dry clothes, even if they were all black, was indeed a blessing. I watched with a jaundiced eye as James blessed them as they departed. The village was like most others. A few thatched mud-built and stone-fronted cottages, randomly clustered together around one slated building – the church – whose belfry towered overall.

I noticed a man jumping up and down, pulling a rope beside the belfry and the bell rang. I blessed myself out of habit. Someone dead, I thought. Then the doors opened and they came out, the women dressed in their best and the men uncomfortable in white starched collars. They doffed their caps to us as we approached. Two women detached themselves from the crowd, jostling each other as they extended their hands in greeting.

'I am Ann,' said the taller of the two. 'I am the parish priest's housekeeper.'

'I am Margot,' said the other. 'I housekeep for the curate.'

They exchanged glances as James introduced us, himself taking the mantle of parish priest. They exchanged triumphant glances to show they would have made the same choice if it was theirs to make. Another group had joined us; this group did not doff their caps and stood aside from the rest. They circled a giant of a man who stood staring at us. James caught his eye and nodded a greeting, but his expression never changed.

We were ushered into the parish priest's house where everything was spick and span. Ann had attached herself to James and was describing with relish the meal she had prepared for us in a loud voice directed at Margot, who was watching her coldly while searching the dresser for signs of dust. Margot looked at me.

'She is full of pride, Father,' she sniffed. 'Wait until you see what I can cook for you,' she added looking down her nose at the glorious spread on the table. The big man had detached himself from his followers, his hand extended towards James. He flinched as the giant squeezed his hand.

'They call me Wexford,' he introduced himself. 'I have no time for priests,' he informed us, 'but I won't bother ye if ye don't bother me.'

'I did not know Wexford was that big,' said James.

I sniggered, and the giant's head turned towards me.

'Laugh if you like,' his hand stuck out towards me, and I took it, 'but anyone who tries to tell me what to do or what to think will end up in the black hole like the bailiff.'

The pressure grew on my hand and I began to return it. Our eyes locked. At some time in the past he might have looked human, even handsome. But now there was little to be seen through the facial hair except the broken nose and three missing teeth that became visible as his lips peeled back with the need to increase the grip on my hand.

'Would you forgive me for throwing the bailiff in the black hole, Father?' he asked.

The pressure mounted. People nudged each other. James kicked me in the shin.

'I would forgive you, my son,' I said, 'but not if you break my fingers.'

Nervous laughter broke out. He released my hand.

'It is time to eat,' declared Ann, disapproval at our talking to the giant dripping from her voice.

'Margot, you can help,' she said sweetly as if conferring an honour on the housekeeper of a mere curate.

The ruffian called Wexford was heading for the door when James put his hand on his arm.

'Will you not join us?'

Wexford was flustered, unprepared for this invitation. He was not used to mingling with the elite of the parish, and said no.

'Perhaps you have no time between killings,' I said sourly.

'There is always room at my table for a selfproclaimed sinner,' James said in his most priestly tone, sitting Wexford down and taking place beside him.

My housekeeper and I looked at one another now. We both felt slighted. I took my place at the table in the lowly place reserved for curates. Wexford was shoving food into his mouth when I remembered the incident with the priests in the hovel. I rose to my feet and proclaimed, 'We will say grace.'

He stopped eating, his breathing and swallowing got mixed up, and he began to choke. James slapped his new friend on the back, and a chunk of meat flew across the table and landed on the sparkling white blouse of a lady across from him, as particles speckled the linen tablecloth that was Ann's pride and joy.

My enjoyment of the spectacle was interrupted as an agitated man burst in.

'That's Ned,' said Margot. 'Mrs O'Grady must be bad.'

Ned looked from James to me and said, 'Thank God you have arrived. There is no time to waste.'

'Attend to that, Fr Tobin,' said James. 'I will say grace.'

He caught my look of revolt and continued, 'We will also sit in a prayer for those that are wet and hungry and without a roof over their heads.'

That settled the question.

'Take me to her, Ned,' I said.

The pony and trap that was the property of Mrs O'Grady was our transport. I remarked how well it was kept as we sped to Mrs O'Grady's, a thatched cottage neatly kept, with hens in the yard and a cow in the paddock behind it. I jumped out and pushed through the half door. Inside were four old women dressed in black, one more feeble than the other.

'Which one of ye is Mrs O'Grady?' I asked.

One of them cackled and pointed to a doorway and returned to laying out the snuff and whiskey for the wake. I entered the room. Light flickered on the wall from the candle under the Sacred Heart picture, beside which stood a glass vase with wilted flowers. Another burned, showing holy water in a bowl with a palm leaf beside the bed in which she lay wasted and clinging to life.

Her eyes were fixed on the door. So great was her need that she tried to rise to greet me. I knelt beside her. She told me of her sins which visibly lightened her load as mine grew heavy. She spoke of her love for Ned and the fear he would be homeless, and on her need to administer her will while keeping her secret.

She took from under her pillow the keys to a tin box I was to take with me. She gripped my shoulder with surprising strength and looked into my eyes.

'Promise me,' she pleaded.

I promised.

'You can tell them to come in now,' she said. The old women and Ned gathered around the bed. Something resembling a smile flitted across her face.

'I am at peace,' she said. 'I give my pony and trap to Fr Tobin. He will need it for his duties.'

She stopped talking and lay back on the bed. Her breath became a rattle. The old crones were looking at me expectantly. I caught the palm spray, dipped it in the holy water and began to chant in the Latin I learned as an altar boy. I hoped it was appropriate as nobody had bothered to tell us what it meant. When I finished they were still looking at me with the same expression.

'Are you not giving her the oil, Father?' one of them prompted.

I searched my pockets in desperation. I must have left it in the trap I concluded, as I made my hurried exit. When I had done the deed, I left Ned to his private grief and drove away in Mrs O'Grady's pony and trap while she sped to heaven with the sign of the cross in axle grease on her forehead.

TORMENT

The drive in the fresh evening air had enhanced my already ravenous hunger. I barged through the door of the parish house, my mouth watering as I remembered the feast that had been laid out for us. It was gone, as were the parishioners. Sitting in front of empty plates were James, Wexford, and his evillooking cohorts. I could smell food and looked around in hope, but all hope was dashed as the Wexford giant lifted one cheek of his seat and let a prolonged fart. And his sneering gap-toothed smile. I was on my way towards him when Margot, who had been cowering in the corner, ran to me.

'I am sorry, Father. Father O'Brien asked them in. Come,' she said, 'I will boil you an egg.'

I left with the mocking laughter of Wexford ringing in my ears. Another egg for breakfast. Then I tackled the pony and called Margot.

'Show me my parish.'

She climbed into the trap beside me.

'Which way first?' I asked.

She pointed towards the parish house. She flicked her shawl over her shoulder and stuck out her jaw. Ann was in the garden, her back turned as we passed, and did not seem to hear the sweet good morning greeting from Margot. I was met with poverty.

Bit by bit, a story emerged from Margot. Wexford and his men would come and take what they wanted. She warned me about saying anything, as the last priests denounced them from the altar and were paraded around the parish, sitting backwards on an ass, and sent on their way.

I hurried back to the village to tell James about his new friend's crimes, only to be told by Ann that he had gone on a mission and I was in charge of the clerical duties.

I said funeral Mass for Mrs O'Grady. Sacrilege, what matter; I was already damned. I mumbled the Latin I had heard at Mass and, although I often wondered about the secret prayers the priest said when he relapsed into silence, I was glad to mimic them now. To touch the chalice, the silver cup, we were told merited instant damnation. It was just that – a silver cup.

As I was not a priest, I reasoned the wine was just wine. They came to me after the burial and told me I was a saint, and that Mrs O'Grady had never looked happier in her long life than she did at the wake. I told them Mrs O'Grady, having no living relatives, had left all to the church, and the church, in turn, had given Ned the house for his long service to his boss. When Sunday came, I denounced Wexford and his cronies from the altar to gasps from the pews.

Then there was the collection. Not much but eggs and vegetables were left, and Margot and myself ate well. Margot, who handled the times for everything like special Masses or baptisms, consulted her calendar and informed me that it was the men's month.

I blinked at her, not understanding. 'The men's month,' she repeated, 'for confession.'

They regaled me with their evil thoughts and indecent acts, mostly committed against themselves. I was fascinated. I asked probing questions. I was aroused like never before. On ladies confessions day it was the same; they just needed more coaxing. I was always sympathetic and gave little penance. But my taste began to harden, and I became tired of stories of self-abuse, even the record-breaking ones. Sins like the farmer who had stolen a ram to start his flock. Now he had many sheep, but he could not return it to gain absolution or he would be labelled a thief. This bored me.

'Give it to the church, my son, and your sins for the past month and the next month will be forgiven.'

I grew impatient with a youth who confided that the previous priest told him he would go blind, and told him it was nonsense. This I knew as I had perfect eyesight. I was changing. I began to eye up Margot despite the fact she had a distinct moustache and mousey hair as befitting a priest's housekeeper. I began to bump into her in the hallway, to look down her blouse when she served my meals. She began to open her buttons and show a little more. Each night I went to bed my need became a living thing in my stomach.

I became intolerant. Sometimes when I gave a sermon I lost control and, fuelled by self-pity, I railed against those in the parish who lived in sin, openly fornication every night. I was turning into Father Watkins. I even used lines from his sermons.

At night I resisted the urge to enter Margot's room and ravish her. Margot had taken to leaving her door open. It had become a ritual as I passed. She would be there at the washstand, naked to the waist. I began to drink every night, the fierce need dulled by alcohol. It was on one of those nights that Margot came to me.

I felt her nakedness on top of mine vaguely, like in a dream. Her heavy breasts floating on my chest, I reached between her legs. She gasped and a shudder ran through her. She was ready, but the alcohol, together with the brush of her moustache on my upper lip, had done for me. I was limp.

'I can't, I can't!' I cried in despair.

She jumped off of me.

'I am sorry, father. I am so ashamed,' she cried. 'Please don't send me away.' And was gone.

I had enhanced my reputation as a holy man and closed the door on my chance of a normal life. My fretful mind questioned was it God or the Devil or both. My body and soul were in torment.

KATHY DOHERTY

I began to reflect on the direction my life was taking; had I not been happier following Molly and the plough up the barren hillside? Work, I threw myself into it. I got Ned to list jobs to be done for the needy, those who had no menfolk, widows and the like. I was on a roof repairing a leak for Mrs Doherty who had a child whose only means of travel was her hands, as she dragged her withered legs behind her. I heard a voice from underneath me saying, 'Are you trying to get closer to God?'

There she was. Kathy Doherty, tall fair-haired and beautiful. She wore clothes that had been scrubbed too often, but on her, they were regal. She was smiling, but the smile did not reach her eyes.

'I brought some stew,' she said. 'Would you like to eat with us?'

I watched as she took a pot from a bag she was carrying and divided it into three. The girl on the floor dragged herself across the floor and sat looking up at me as her plate was lowered to her. Her eyes met mine and held them.

'Will you cure me, Father?' she asked.

My eyes fell away from hers in shame, the likes of which I had never felt.

'Leave Father alone,' her mother scolded her, as she sat beside me. 'I don't know what I would do without my daughters.'

Looking into my shamed face, she said, 'I would like you to say a prayer for my daughter.' She paused and added, 'both my daughters.' Her eyes locked with Kathy's, who flushed and rose.

'I have to go now,' she said, putting the pot back into the bag.

'Can I walk with you?' I asked.

'Please yourself,' she replied.

Her mother watched from the door as we left and her invalid daughter waved from the floor. We set off in silence, my mind returning to the disabled girl asking if I could cure her.

'She asks them all that, don't let it upset you.'

I looked at her startled. How had she known what I was thinking? Kathy was looking straight ahead as she spoke.

'We both know life is not like that.'

We walked on in silence. I began to wonder why I had not seen her before.

'You are going to ask me why you have not seen me in church.' She was at it again.

'Well, yes,' I said. 'I would have remembered.'

'The last priest told me to come back when I have repented. I have not repented.'

'I am not like the previous priest,' I said. 'Look around you.'

We both did. It was high summer. Birds sang, and butterflies and bees flitted from flower to flower, the tall pine trees shading us from the sun.

'There is no church as good as this. You can talk to me here.'

She told me her story matter-of-factly. A father who died young, a sister crippled, she worked for a strong farmer as a maid by day and a mistress by night. The farmer's wife had presented him with two fine sons, declared her job as a wife done, and turned to religion. Hence his need for a mistress, and it meant Kathy's family ate well.

'I have to keep my job,' she said.

'What do you want from me?' I asked.

'Understanding would be kind,' she answered.

'I understand,' I said. 'But do you understand?'

For the second time in an hour, I had to confront what I was.

'You will get pregnant. The farmer will throw you out. The nuns will take the baby.'

My voice was angry; now, she was backing away from me. I sounded just like the others. But I could not stop. Something buried deep inside of me was coming out.

'You will leave a child, just like my mother did, who will always question why. Was he loved or hated, or just a piece of garbage to be disposed of?' I stood there shaken.

40

She came to me and held me, and we were like brother and sister.

As she left, she turned and said, 'Don't worry, there is a woman in the village who takes care of that.'

One more damned than the other, I thought.

She came to church after that. In confession, she told me in detail what he did to her, and I understood. Then she told me she thought about me when he was doing it, and it made it better, and she hung her sins around my neck, and with it the knowledge that she was mine for the asking.

THE LOST SHEEP AND THE BLACK SHEEP

'BAA, BAA'

I woke thinking I had dreamed of sheep, but I still could hear their bleating. I looked out; the field behind the house was full of sheep.

'Margot,' I asked 'where did they come from?'

'They were there when I woke. I heard stories,' she added and stopped.

'Go on,' I said.

'I heard stories that forgiveness and indulgences were given for the return of stolen sheep.' I remembered during the chaos of confession that I had promised such. They must have been stealing from each other for years.

I walked out through them, and I was reminded of a biblical figure as they flowed around me. Ned was called and asked to draw a list of the neediest to whom the sheep would be donated. James came and went at will, and I noticed an increasing number of strange characters began to appear at the church and went to confession only to James. I would see them in the company of the brutish Wexford fellow who gave me the eye as he passed.

Margot and Ann no longer pretended to be friends. They would outline the feast they were preparing, each trying to produce a meal of such quality that the other could not possibly match. Margot pointed out the excellent work I was doing looking after the poorest of the parish, and proclaimed that I should be the parish priest and James should be the curate. Ann responded by pointing out that James should be bishop, as he now had converted known blackguards to the church, and was it not said there was a great celebration in heaven when a lost sheep had been found.

Then, one Sunday, the lost sheep all turned up at Mass with the black sheep called Wexford sitting in the front seat with legs splayed grinning up at me. You could have heard a pin drop as I left the sacristy. I mounted the steps to the pulpit, my eyes fixed on the loathsome brute. I addressed my parishioners.

'We have today murderers, thieves and vagabonds who have no place in this place of worship. I call on them to leave this place of God.'

All the time I was talking, I was looking directly at Wexford who was scratching his beard and smiling his gap-toothed sneer. I expected this to provoke him, and I would relish any hurt I could inflict as I threw him out. The thought that I might not be able niggled at the back of my mind, but the prospect of wiping that grin off his face outweighed any fear.

'But you forgave us, Father,' Wexford said in a mocking, wheedling voice.

'What?' I thundered.

'We returned all we stole. Did you not notice all the sheep in the priest's field?'

My mind grappled with this problem as I remembered my blanket dispensation.

'Forgiveness for thievery, yes,' I cried, 'but not for murder.'

'What of the bailiff you threw into the black hole?' I crowed in triumph, my face reddening with temper at having been outsmarted by the brute.

He turned his back to me and spread his hands and addressed my worshippers. He climbed out. My flock erupted in laughter. Murderer he might not be, but murderer I would be as I climbed down from the pulpit heading for him.

James appeared from nowhere, grabbed my arm and said, 'I will finish for you, Father.'

After I cooled down and the crowd dispersed, we walked home together, questions still in my mind.

'Where,' I asked, 'did Wexford get the sheep?'

'Do you not remember our stock?'

'Yes,' I said.

'Well, I sent Wexford to get them back.'

We walked on as I mulled over this information.

'But,' I said, 'we did not have that many sheep.'

'Does Wexford look like a man that can count?' James asked.

And I felt better and went home.

REALITY

Margot started the minute I got home.
'How could he do that to you, and you running the parish on your own?'

'That, Ann, is behind this.'

'Go to Father O'Brien and demand the respect you deserve.'

'I will,' I declared.

Her hands were on her hips.

I sighed.

'After supper,' I answered. I knew I would get no peace until I did.

There was a knock on the door. Ann stood there.

'Well, it's lady muck herself,' Margot exclaimed.

'Father O'Brien wants to see you, Father Tobin,' Ann said, ignoring Margot.

'Give Ann a slice of your lovely cake,' I advised Margot, and left hurriedly.

Inspired by Margot, I berated James for his lack of interest in running the parish, filled with my importance. I felt my work was such that the parish priest should be at my side, not parading around with the likes of Wexford. I concluded that it was too much to expect that I could continue as before.

James contemplated me.

'We have sheltered here while the clouds of war gather. All around us those clouds will soon burst and the weak will be washed away. Wexford and his men have been stealing sheep on my instructions. Faith, Hope and Charity went to Lordy for protection. Lordy sent soldiers to recover the sheep; a simple job, as sheep are easy to track through trees and brush. Those men never returned.'

He paused.

'You killed them!' I exclaimed.

'We needed their horses, we needed their uniforms, and we needed their silence,' he explained.

'They will send an army next time,' I blurted as my world fell around me.

'Yes,' he said, 'they will send an army.'

'Wexford's men began to fight over the horses,' James continued. 'I promised them a horse each. We dressed ourselves in our stolen uniforms and raided Lord Woodford's, tied up the sentries and made off with a stable of horses. Wexford sent a man to acquaint Lordy that I, James Landers, was behind the disappearance of his men, and we were based in this village and expected a share of the reward, while Wexford approached the royalist Lord Woodford with information that the stolen horses were to be used in a surprise attack to be launched through our village within days.

'The people must be warned,' I said, fragments of decency emerging with the realisation that our cruel deception could bring about the slaughter of innocents.

I climbed the steps to the belfry and rang the bell. I stood before them for the last time as their priest. I told them of a great evil that was coming. I borrowed from Father Watkins' speech before he disappeared and told them I would miss them. Tears came to my eyes as I felt it to be true. I said to them that at first light they should take food and hide in the woods until safe to return.

They crowded around me as they bade me farewell.

Margot pleaded to come with me. I assured her where I was going she would not want to be, in this life or the next. Ann embraced her, difference forgotten in mutual dismay, as they too faced reality.

OLD SLEEPY

The morning saw James and his ruffians saddled up and preparing to leave the now deserted village. I was glumly accepting the fact I was one of them.

'One last task,' James announced. 'I need someone reliable to remain to ring the bell when Lord Stapleton's army is sighted, to give Lord Woodford time to set his ambush.'

'That will be me, I suppose,' Wexford said, starting to dismount.

'Over my dead body,' I said, my mouth being faster than my brain. I realised this as he swung back into the saddle, giving me that gapped smile that annoyed me so much.

'Leave him the fastest horse,' James ordered.

'We will leave him Old Sleepy,' Wexford said, 'nothing will catch him.'

I saw one of his cronies nudge the other and was about to ask questions, but they were looking over my shoulder.

Turning around, I saw Kathy Doherty walking down the road, and as I watched her all thoughts of horses went out of my head.

James rode off followed by his new friends, leaving Old Sleepy tied to the church door. I woke him as I passed and saw the white of an eye role in annoyance; he swished his tail and kicked at flies, although the morning was cold and I could not see any. I was pleased, as he was a large lump of bone and muscle, and the view from the belfry was such I would be long gone before Lordy's soldiers entered the village.

I heard her footsteps on the stairs. It was Kathy with a basket.

'Something to eat before you go,' she said. Her eyes were red and teary. 'What will I do without you?'

'There will be other priests,' I replied.

'But not like you.'

'No,' I admitted, 'not like me.'

She took out some brown bread and bacon, and as I reached out for it, she grasped my hand.

'Sit with me.'

I sat.

'I want to say goodbye,' she said. 'I dream about you and what it would be like.'

'As do I,' I admitted.

'Then take me,' her eyes bright with desire.

'I cannot,' I said.

'Because you are a priest?'

'Because you are my friend,' I said.

50

I was her friend and knew our lives ran on similar lines; we would do what we had to to survive. I knew if I touched her when she discovered what I was it would hurt the part of her the farmer could not reach, and she would slip even closer to what she was called behind her back.

Lights flickered and flashed around the belfry, and just for a moment I thought it was a sign from God that at last I had done the right thing. I jumped up; they were entering the village, sun flashing on steel my halo. I rang the bell.

'Stay there, they will follow me,' I advised Kathy. 'Remember me with kindness.'

It would look good on a headstone, I thought.

I grabbed the bell rope and slid down. As my hands burned, the bell gave one last lament for its makebelieve priest.

When the peels reached them, they quickened their pace. I grabbed Old Sleepy's reins. He was displeased to be woken, and a pair of hoofs flashed past my nose. In desperation, I gripped his mane and launched myself in the general direction of the saddle. Bared teeth flashed at my rear end, but my flailing boot caught him in the mouth and he began to gallop. My relief was short-lived as he had swung around and was heading for the soldiers, who had lowered their lances to receive me. I pulled frantically on the reins and he spun around.

For a while, I hung sideways, but I stayed on. I heard an order shouted to 'Get that priest!'

Then another shouted, 'That's no priest, that's James' bastard brother.'

The black soutane was catching in the wind so I tore it off. I crested a rise and, in battle formation in front of me, were my Catholic saviours. Then I heard a cry. 'That's my horse under the thieving Protestant leading them.'

I pulled the reins and we ran down the rapidly closing gauntlet, pursued shouts of 'that's my horse!' Ahead was a wall of brush, and behind that the forest. With a wall of pointed steel bearing down on us from both sides, and fuelled by mutual cowardice, Old Sleepy left the ground and crashed through the brush. I saw his owner carried off on the point of a lance as his horse disappeared under the wave of war.

I heard a battle cry from my right and glimpsed a group of Woodford's men run from the trees to cut off Stapleton's retreat. I did not dwell on this as we dashed through the trees at breakneck speed. Then, I noticed Old Sleepy went for the high branches, but horse and rider were intact as we came to an exausted halt. When our breath returned, I nudged the horse away from here. Soon the trees grew sparse and we were in grassland. We turned for home.

THE REWARD

They were where we had agreed to meet, in the woods overlooking our old home. I tied Old Sleepy to a tree and walked cautiously towards their camp. They sat in a group talking and laughing. I decided to rest behind a tree and listen to their discourse in the hope I could find common cause with my new companions. Tales of thievery and debauchery were commonplace, with a general agreement on how their fortunes had changed since Wexford and James had become partners. We went from tramps on foot to soldiers on horseback.

'Speaking of horses,' one interrupted, tears of laughter already smudging the dirt on his face as he recounted the story of the horse left at the church. When Wexford said nothing would catch him, I nearly gave the game away by laughing. I tried, and I still have the bite marks on my arse; Wexford himself tried, and it kicked him into the bushes. They were still laughing as I burst into the camp. I made a beeline for the storyteller who, interpreting my rage as I made for him, said 'shite'. I stopped with my nose almost touching his.

'Where is he?'

'Shite,' he repeated with less alarm, pointing towards the trees. I got the smell before I saw him, and knew it for what it was, diarrhoea. My spirit lifted. He saw me coming too late as I shoved him down into the stinking mess underneath him. I left before he could get to his feet. I found James looking down at the great house.

'Glad to see you,' he said. 'How long have we got?'

'A day at the most.' He knew as I did the battle would not last long. 'They got a crop,' I observed, looking at the field I had ploughed in another lifetime.

'The gate is closed,' James observed. 'How many men are left down there?' he mused.

'Does it matter?' I pointed out. 'With the gates closed we can't get in.'

'We can get in,' James assured me. 'Now getting out, that could be a problem. What's that smell?' he finished. I smelled the air.

'That,' I concluded, 'smells like your new partner.' Wexford joined us looking daggers at me, but said nothing.

'We go in tonight as we planned.' The uniforms taken from Lordy's men were again put to use. 'Tie us up,' James ordered. Wexford picked up a rope and advanced towards James, who backed away and said, 'Get one of the others to do it.' The slight was not lost on Wexford, who glared at me and handed the rope to one of his men. When James was secured, Wexford said, 'Him too', pointing at me.

'No one is tying me,' I said, grabbing a sword that was hanging on a tree with the stolen uniforms. 'Then you can't come with us,' Wexford said. 'They will know you.'

'Put a uniform on and pull down the helmet; it will be dark; we may not meet anyone who knows you.' James settled the argument. We rode up to the gate, nine uniformed soldiers of which I was one, and one tied prisoner, James. The sentry opened a hatch in the gate.

'Who goes there?'

'Sergeant Gorey,' Wexford replied, 'with a prisoner.'

'I don't know you. Where are the others?'

'The last I saw of them they were gathering sheep; but we have the real prize – Landers. He has a reward on his head, at least that is what he told us as we were about to add him to the other corpses.'

'I know him. Bring him to the gate.' Wexford lifted James from his horse and caught his face and held it to the gate.

'That is Landers,' the sentry said, 'fifty coins worth; but I have orders to admit no strangers.' 'We have orders to return to the main army. We must collect reward now,' Wexford demanded. 'Orders are orders,' the sentry said. 'Tie Landers to the gate. I will see you get the reward.'

'Look at me,' Wexford demanded. 'Where on me do you see 'idiot' written?'

James chimed in, 'Sergeant, Sir, I will give you one hundred coins for my freedom, and another hundred for the horse.' Another face appeared at the hatch. I recognised the soldier with the peas. Wexford inspected James.

'Where would you get two hundred coins?'

'In a belt around my waist,' James said. 'Untie me, and we will do the deal.'

Wexford untied James who reached under his priest's garb and produced a belt. Wexford grabbed the belt and hefted it – more than two hundred.

'There. You have a deal. On your way.'

'Wait. You can't do that to us. If Lordy finds out we let Landers go free, he will have our heads.'

'Look at me,' Wexford said. 'Do I look like someone who cares?'

'You can have it all,' the pea player was getting desperate. 'The belt and the reward.'

'Do I look like someone who goes back on a deal?'

'Yes,' the sentry said honestly. James had started to slip away when Wexford's huge hand grabbed him by the neck.

'We are not greedy,' Wexford said. 'We will give you half.' The pea pusher's eyes fell on the money belt.

'Half of the reward,' Wexford added frostily, 'and my men have not eaten today.' The gate swung open. We dismounted in the courtyard where more soldiers than I would have liked loitered and there would be others asleep. We went through the kitchen again, past Martha's horrified gaze, past maids loading food and drink on trays. The shell player went in; first I heard Lordy's voice asking him what he wanted. He did not sound pleased.

'We have Landers, Sir.'

'Bring him in,' Lordy's voice had changed to pleased. We filed in. Wexford stood beside me with James on a rope. I sneaked a glance; six prosperous couples sat at the table.

'This man,' said Lordy pointing at James, 'could have had all this. Look at him now.'

'The reward,' Wexford said.

'How dare you interrupt me,' Lordy said.

'The reward,' Wexford said again in the same even tone. Lordy stared at the big brute and decided that manners were not to be expected.

'A yes, the reward. Fifty coins, I believe.'

'One hundred,' Wexford corrected in the same even voice. Lordy was getting annoyed again. 'That was for two. I have two,' Wexford's hand snaked around my neck, and I felt the prick of a dagger under my chin as he lifted the helmet.

'A hundred it is,' said Lordy as he disappeared. He reappeared with a pouch that jingled and threw it to Wexford who caught it deftly but caused pressure on the dagger. A trickle of blood ran down my neck.

'Thank you, my Lord,' Wexford said in a rare show of manners. 'They are yours now.' The blade came away from my neck, and the rope of James. I drew my sword. I was mad now with everyone, but as I looked around, the shell player and his partner were pinned against the wall. Lordy and his guests seemed frozen in horror. Wexford, on the other hand, had bolted the door, moved to the table, and was helping himself to food with his back turned. I poked him with my sword. He kept eating. I poked him harder.

'I was wrong,' he admitted. 'I knew better than to expect more.' I put away my sword. 'I thought you were worthless,' he added. Wexford stood up from the table,

57

still chewing; a sure indication that some of the food had escaped the clutches of his beard.

'Now, your Lordship,' said Wexford. 'What had you in store for the Landers pair?'

'Yes,' James inquired. 'What had you in store for us?'

'Why, nothing,' Lordy said.

'You would say that now, would you not?' I observed.

'Ahh, come on, your Lordship, what would you have done to the big one? Pluck out his eyes maybe?'

'Why, nothing,' Lordy replied.

'Cut off his extremities?' suggested Wexford enjoying himself.

'No,' Lordy protested. The answers were not suiting Wexford; he produced a dagger.

'Can I?' he asked James.

'Yes,' James said, 'but don't kill him.' Lordy wisely did not wait.

'I told you the truth,' he insisted. 'I was going to hand ye over to the papal army as an act of diplomacy.' I was losing track of the conversation.

'Why?' asked James.

'Blasphemy, sacrilege, murder. I have in my possession letters to Bishop Watkins from the housekeepers of two priests. The letters were praising their work, one with the poor and the other with the dregs of humanity.' He paused to look at Wexford. 'In less enlightened times, his would be acclaimed as a miracle, as I had hung both. After all, both sides have to protect the faith. I also believe their methods of disposal of such as ye are much more inventive.'

Wexford looked at James, who shrugged. Wexford said, 'Right answer, your Lordship,' before pushing him aside. Lordy walked over to his chair and pulled it back.

'This is what you came for, is it not?' James walked over to the chair and sat down.

'Do you feel it?' Lordy asked. 'The responsibility. I had to make decisions sitting in that chair between a decadent, priest-ridden royalty or the parliament. I chose the parliament. I believe in it. Your father decided to end his life on that chair. He knew his day was done. The O'Neil's, all that's left of your kind, will be dragged into this war. I can tell you now his lands are already promised to supporters on both sides. People like my guests who pay the soldiers will reap the spoils.' Lordy was getting back his composure. 'While you are on that chair, you reflect where it sits, and what will happen when my army returns.'

'Your army is no more, your Lordship,' I informed him. Lordy looked at me.

'Imbecile' was all he said.

'That sums him up,' agreed Wexford like he knew what it meant, before walking into Lordy's private chamber. James caught the eye of one of Wexford's men who was watching the courtyard. Who nodded.

'Your army has returned your Lordship.' There was a knock at the door. Lordy looked at James. 'Answer it,' James ordered.

'My Lord, there are people at the gate seeking entry.'

'Who are they?' Lordy asked.

'Survivors, sir, and a group of peasants.'

'Let them in,' a shocked Lordy said without prompting. Wexford walked out of Lordy's chamber with a bag that jingled, but what drew my eye was his leather breeches it stopped six inches above his ankles, and his arse was jammed into the other end.

'Nice,' I said as he passed. The peasants were the remainder of Wexford's men who burst into the house and locked the doors behind them, but not before I escorted Martha and the maids outside for their safety. Martha, the closest to a mother I had ever known, wanted to talk to me, but I had other things on my mind. I went back up the stairs to the dining room. The guests were now serving Wexford's uncouth ruffians to everyone's amusement but theirs. Lordy was in a huff. He had retaken his seat and refused to move, despite chicken legs and leftovers being pelted at him. James had detached himself and was looking out the window. I joined him. After a moment of silence, I ventured, 'What now?'

'Wait and See.' We waited, and in the morning could see Woodford's army camped outside the gate.

THE BATTLE OF LANDERS' HALL

We stood at the battlements looking out at Woodford's army. Two rows of muskets backed up by a row of lancers. On a vantage point behind them, two coaches, both with matching horses grazing on the lush grass. An officer who had been talking to the occupants called a soldier. The soldier attached a white flag to his spear and rode with the officer to the gate. James, Wexford, Lordy and I went out to meet them. The officer pulled a parchment from under his arm and began to read.

'Lord Stapleton to surrender to Lord Woodford, to answer to the charge of treason and the murder of two priests. Those lands to be added to the Woodford estate.'

James replied, 'I am James Landers of Landers' Hall. I hold these lands by right of conquest. However, I would offer Lord Stapleton and this property to Lord Woodford for a fair reward.'

'I shall convey your offer to his Lordship,' the officer replied. He wheeled his horse and rode back up the hill. When he returned, he produced the parchment again.

'Lord Stapleton – treason and murder. James Landers and John Landers – blasphemy, sacrilege, horse stealing.'

James replied, 'It would be in your interest to urge your Lordship to accept my offer. My men would resent killing without reward. Return at noon, and as a sign of good faith, Lord Stapleton will be outside the gates.' The officer went, leaving a very unhappy Lordy.

'I will pay you to fight with me.'

'With what?' James pointed out, 'What you have we have already taken. When you go outside the gate, you will be armed leading your men. I have just bought three hours for the promise of your head, now show me your armoury.'

The armoury was impressive. His guests had brought support in the form of pistols and muskets. 'Now,' Lordy said to James, 'all we need is a hundred men to use them.'

'Twenty on muskets,' James was thinking out loud, 'all loaded and primed. Twenty loading as they fired. Wexford, get twenty of your men and everyone out here – guests, maids, wounded. Form teams.' Lordy began organising the groups. I followed James and Wexford back onto the wall as we contemplated the vastly superior force lined up against us. I unhelpfully observed, 'This was the bit you were doubtful about, getting out again.'

'I expected Lordy's army to have reduced their number,' James admitted. 'Lordy sent a weak force. We may also have to confront the possibility they are well-led.'

Lordy had his teams organised with powder and ball, spaced along the front wall at each side of the gate, ready to load for a line of Wexford's men on the wall. James nodded his pleasure at Lordy.

'Now saddle every horse and keep them in the stables with your remaining men. When they attack after the first wave, I will open the gate, and you will charge out. Bear to your left; that will draw the lancers. When that happens, swing back to the cover of the muskets on the wall.'

'What then?' Lordy asked.

'Then this battle will be over,' James said.

Lordy said, 'If I were out there, I would sit and wait for a cannon. What makes you think they will attack?

'They will attack,' James said with certainty.

Noon came. The soldier with the white flag and the officer rode towards the gate. James and Wexford, Lordy and I went to the entrance to meet them.

'I trust you convinced Lord Woodford to make a substantial offer for my prize,' James inquired. 'No,' the officer snapped. 'We came for Lord Stapleton as agreed.'

'Lord Stapleton informs me he is expecting a section of his army to return shortly, and I should not be too hasty.' The officer was only half listening; he was looking around the courtyard, and all that was visible were a few women.

'They are dead,' said the officer.

'You were there?' probed James.

'Yes,' the officer admitted.

'Did you follow Lord Woodford into battle?' James asked. The officer snorted.

'You led them,' James concluded. The officer's air of indifference was beginning to fade.

'I came as you requested for Lord Stapleton. Lord Stapleton has made a counteroffer for my services which you have given me no option but to accept James replied.

'Would it be possible that without you those out there would be undisciplined rabble?' James asked. The officer was worried now.

'I came here under a white flag.'

'You should have carried it,' James pointed out. 'Have you no honour?' He had begun to back his horse. 'Blasphemy, sacrilege, murder,' James reminded him. Wexford pulled two pistols from behind his back and blasted him out of the saddle.

We watched as the soldier with the white flag galloped past the musketeers through the line of lancers to the coaches. He pointed excitedly in our direction. The occupant jumped out of the coach, jumping around with temper and shouting at the musketeers who rushed at the wall; they could not climb a gate they could not open. Lordy's men on the walls opened fire, dropped the musket to the loaders and picked up another. The attackers caught in the open were taking severe losses, and began to pull back their weapons empty. James gave the signal, the gate opened. Lordy and his men galloped out. They cut a swathe through the musketeers; the lancers went to their aid. Lordy and his men fled in front of them. James signalled again and the gates swung open. This time it was our turn. We hit the cobbles at the gallop. Wexford's men formed a loose line at each side of us as we drove through. Some of them had reloaded, and horses and men fell on both sides of us. Still, we galloped on. In front of me, two lancers were levelling their lances. I opened my mouth to scream with fear or defiance, and it came out, 'Landers'. Then, something strange happened. Old Sleepy, who had been biting and kicking at the musketeers as we passed, laid back his ears, bared his teeth and charged at the first lancer. I desperately parried the thrust of the first lancer; knowing the second one was heading for my breastbone, Sleepy crashed into the first horse sending him over backwards under the legs of the second lancer's horse, who went down; his rider trampled under Sleepy's hoofs. Then, we were through. The coaches with the bishop and Lord Woodford were ours; the battle of Landers' Hall was over.

OF FLESH
AND BLOOD

We paraded Lord Woodford under our sword through his circling army. Lordy had made it back to the cover of the wall; what remained of his men were gathered around him.

'Why?' James prodded Woodford. 'Why? I gave you Lord Stapleton's army, I offered an alliance; you wanted it all.'

'It was him,' Woodford said, pointing at the bishop. Wexford prodded the bishop, giving him his gap-toothed smile. The bishop flinched away from the sword.

'You two are destined for hellfire,' he bleated. Lord Woodford agreed that 'hanging was too good for ye.'

'The land for Lord Woodford, the house for a bishop and the rope for those that made it possible,' James said grimly. 'We will go back to the hall. We have a lot to discuss. That means you too, Lordy.'

'Not as your prisoner,' snarled Lordy.

'That is your decision to make. I tire of you all. Before you decide, you should look over your head.' Twenty muskets were pointing in his direction. Lordy cursed and threw his weapons down. Lordy's men were locked in the barracks. I walked back to the hall. James took his seat at the head of the table. He sat, waiting for his hands on his head. They sat watching him, two warring lords and a bishop and Lordy's guests. Wexford burst in.

'Six of my men are dead. The others are outside and they want blood.'

'Let them enter,' James conceded. They filled the hall. Wexford said, 'They have lost friends, and they are angry.' James caught a pistol and banged it on the table.

'I will hear every man. I want them to tell me of the friends they lost and the justice they require.' They came forwards one at a time. They were telling stories of eviction, persecution for petty theft of food, and endless stories of poverty. They remembered their dead comrades, and spoke of the dependants they'd left behind. After each had spoken, James asked them what justice did they require. When they had come to the last man, I, for my part, had to confront the fact that they were people just like me, swept along by the tide of circumstances, not of their own making. James had been taking notes and, after some scribbling, set aside his quill.

'In front of me, I have your preference for justice for your fallen comrades. Most want Lord Woodford hanged; some of you want both. I, James, continue to have reason to want both. Lord Stapleton has already hung me, and

Lord Woodford wished to be more efficient and, aided by Bishop Watkins, who you want to free, more inventive. I have listened to your tales of our fallen friends. They are no longer here to share in our spoils. Wexford, give the men their share of the coins, and place on the table in front of me the six shares for our fallen friends. Then break out the wine. We will have an auction; the proceeds to go to their kinfolk.' James pointed to one of the guest's wives. 'You stand up,' he ordered; she remained sitting. 'Refusing to cooperate carries a fine of five shillings,' James explained helpfully.

'Stand up,' snarled her husband. She stood, having shot her husband a murderous look. I thought he had already paid too much for her, as all her bulges were in the wrong place.

'One shilling,' came a voice from within our packed comrades, causing raucous laughter.

'I have one shilling from one of my officers with good taste,' lied James without a blush. The woman glared at her husband.

'Five shillings,' he ground out.

'Sold to her loving husband for five shillings,' James banged the table. 'Your name, sir?'

'Rutherford.'

'Mr Rutherford back here with five shillings, or you will be granted a rather messy divorce.'

'I only wanted the broach she is wearing,' James' officer underbidder blustered as his company tormented him. James pulled the broach from the woman's blouse and threw it to him.

'Be careful with that, it has a point.' To more laughter. 'Next,' James called, pointing at a rather snooty woman who had been regarding the proceedings with disdain. She stood, smiling coldly at James.

'Five shillings. I suppose,' she surmised.

'If that's all you think you are worth,' James replied. She turned her cold gaze on her husband who stuttered, 'Ten shillings.'

'I would have thought you were worth more,' James prompted.

'Thank you,' she said, eying her husband again.

'Fifteen,' he agrees. 'Sold. Fifteen shillings.' The next one was a stunner; tall, black haired, green eyes; everything matched. She rose without being asked, walked the length of the table, twirled, looked defiantly at James as she passed. She stood, hands on hips facing her husband.

'Five shillings,' he muttered.

'What?' James said. 'Only five for this magnificent creature?

'Ten is all I have,' he pleaded.

'What?' she said. 'You told me you were the son of a duke.'

'I am,' he said, 'but he is broke too. I came to Ireland to make my fortune, not to lose what I have.' I heard a voice beside me say, 'Fifteen shillings'. It was Wexford. I started to laugh, but shut up when I saw the look in his eyes. I saw that look in a starving dog once when I fed it. Wexford pulled a heap of coins out of his pocket and began feverishly counting. Lord Stapleton's money no doubt. Shock washed across James' face and was gone. James cast his eye over the coins in front of Wexford.

'I have fifteen in cash from a perfect man.' The black-haired woman was looking at Wexford, horrified; her mouth hung open in shock, but she was still cursed by her beauty. Her shocked eyes swung towards Rutherford. Rutherford cast a furtive eye in the direction of his wife and offered eighteen. Wexford was desperate, as he added the last stack to the three in front of him.

'Twenty shillings,' he announced. James looked at Rutherford.

'Not another word out of you,' Rutherford's wife snarled, 'or you will be back in the gutter where I found you.' The sales item was not happy. 'Well, what about the rest of ye?' her temper was rising. 'I listened to your big promises while I serviced ye in the gentleman's club in London. Under the orders of my husband, my high-class pimp.' All hell broke loose. The women attacked the sales item or their husbands, whichever was nearest, to the amusement of our companions. James fired the pistol he had been using as a gavel. All stopped and looked at him.

'Wexford, go to their rooms. Take everything of value and, Wexford, take her with you.' Wexford grabbed his prize. If he had a tail, it would have been wagging. 'The sale of flesh has concluded; the sale of blood will now commence. What am I bid for Lord Woodford?' They looked at one another, their anger dulled by previous entertainment.

'Well, have I no offer,' a man stepped forward, 'lost my best friend. One shilling, I have.' James said, 'Any advance on one? No increase on one? Come on. One will only buy his little finger. Going once.' James paused. 'Lord Stapleton, would you explain to Lord Woodford that he does not get the shilling for his little finger, I do.' There was a burst of laughter all round. 'Little finger going soon,' James warned. Woodford was looking from James to Stapleton. Lord Stapleton looked at James.

'Rather takes from your victory, Landers. This man is a fool.'

'Little finger going twice,' James rose his gavel.

'I Lord stapleton on behalf of Lord Woodford, I would offer thirty shillings to retain his finger.' There was a loud cheer.

'Thank you, your Lordship. I just wanted to show my men his life has a value; his blood has none.' Too much merriment. Woodford's pieces were all retained, and Lord Woodford was led to the wall to tell his army to return home to collect his ransom, or his pieces would go to the underbidders. Lord Stapleton began to clap.

'Excellent performance. I have just witnessed a bloodthirsty mob turned from their vengeful path, induced to laugh at lords, and shown their dependants would benefit on their demise – all within an apparently mindless act of folly.'

TO HELL OR TO
ULSTER

I watched as Wexford heaped the riches of the house onto the table.

'Well, now we know you are just a common thief.' Lordy was on his high horse again.

'This coming from a man who wanted me to help steal a country,' observed James. 'A man whose very life hangs on the whim of a common thief.' Lordy was stung.

'I never needed you to steal a country. The greatest army this country has ever seen has already landed. They will by now have occupied or besieged every town within miles of Dublin. Then they will swing south, taking every port and town along the way. When O'Neill is isolated, who will stand with him? The likes of him,' he pointed at Lord Woodford, 'who by that time will have changed his colours.

Or him,' he indicated Bishop Watkins, 'who will show support by praying, but not so close to the action this time.

'How do you know these things?' James asked.

'Because I helped plan them,' Lordy proclaimed.

'The papal army will stand by him,' Bishop Watkins broke into the conversation.

'The Papal army,' mocked Lordy, 'I have heard waits for manna from heaven to feed it before it sails.'

'It will sail,' Bishop Watkins retorted. 'Every diocese has given all for this armada.'

'All?' prompted Wexford, poking the bishop.

'All,' the Bishop replied, moving away from his tormenter.

'Lord Woodford will pay a ransom; the bishop will go free,' James reminded Wexford. What, Stapleton, is your offer?'

'Your life,' snapped Lordy, 'and a position as my estate manager.'

'You offered me that just before you hung me,' James pointed out.

'I may have acted in haste,' admitted Lordy, 'but I was right was I not? You are a dangerous man. I need men like you, and think of the good you could do. You understand them out there. I may not be perfect, but you have just seen my guests. There are hundreds of them; sons of lords, bastards of lords, soldiers of fortune, every cutthroat from the gutters of England are descending on Ireland. Soon there will be no Landers, no O'Neills walking on their land. They will be under it, or slaves to the likes of those you have just seen. You have few options,' Lordy was becoming encouraged by his logic. 'Me or Ulster,' Lordy concluded.

'When this army that you speak of comes this way, how uneasy would lie my head,' James countered.

'It seems we are bound for Ulster,' Bishop Watkins interjected, 'whatever route you take, you are bound for hell.'

Bound for hell. The sentence sent a chill down my spine the like of which I would welcome in the fires of hell. I could have been killed in the fracas; where then would I have ended up? I began to examine my conscience. I had not killed anyone nor had I stolen anything, I reassured myself. I had, however, to confront the fact I had performed the duties of a priest with no formal training. That did not sound too bad, but in the back of my mind I seemed to remember there were some sins that only a bishop could forgive, and it was possible, even probable, that mine fell into that category. My eyes locked on Bishop Watkins. He sat at a table beside Wexford who was feeding titbits to the striking woman, who seemed to have recovered from her previous shock. I noted the bishops face was set in an expression that did not suggest a mood of forgiveness. Wine. I went downstairs. Martha rushed over to me.

'I must talk to you,' she said.

'Not now,' I told her. 'I am preparing for confession. Find me a bottle of the best wine.' Armed with the bottle, I went back up the stairs. Pouring a mug full, I sat down beside the bishop, pushing the mug towards him, and giving him my most subservient smile. I whispered, 'I need forgiveness.' He had begun to drink, but slowly lowered the mug.

'What?' he thundered.

'Forgiveness? For what?' This time, it was Wexford from the other side of the bishop.

'You know what,' I snarled. 'Taking the place of a priest.'

'What?' this time it was the bishop, as wine dribbled from his open mouth.

'I thought you were going to confess to humping Moira Doherty,' Wexford said, sounding disappointed.

'I did not hump Moira Doherty. I said I was only sorry I left her sister in such a state.'

'What? this time, the Bishop again.

'She thought I could cure her,' I explained. 'She begged me to do it.'

'What?' it was Wexford this time. 'You humped the cripple?' He was looking at me, giving me his gap-toothed smile, as his dark-haired companion leaned over to view me. The bishop was getting the picture.

'You are looking for forgiveness, my son. You held your bishop at knifepoint, impersonated a man of the cloth, countless incidences of heresy and blasphemy, dubious relationships with women who believed you could perform a miracle. You are fortunate that nobody is beyond God's mercy. What you must do to repent is come with me when I leave here. I will take you to a place where you will be tied to a stake and burned.' Wexford laughed, taking the wine and filling a cup for his doxy.

'Have a mug of wine with us,' offered the black-haired woman.

'Yes,' Wexford agreed. 'Forget about the bishop. He only wants to send you to Hell.'

'Pre-cooked, darling,' the black-haired beauty added. Their laughter followed me as I walked away in disgust.

The next morning, the gates were opened to admit two of Lord Woodford's tenants. The ransom was handed over, and we released the bishop and Lord Woodford. As they left, a delegation of Lordy's tenants approached the gates; Faith, Hope and Charity were prominent amongst them. I guided them up the stairs to the great hall. James was seated in Lordy's chair. Lordy and his male guests were tied securely to a line of chairs against the wall.

'Welcome to Landers' Hall,' James invited. 'Sit,' he ordered. Faith, Hope and Charity looked sheepish and began to apologise. James quickly silenced them.

'We have no time to dwell on the past. Lord Stapleton has caused me to embark on a career to which I am perhaps better suited. Soon we will leave, and you the tenants can judge Lord Stapleton. He can explain to ye why the priests were hung, and give you reasons why he should not be.'

James waited; no one spoke.

'Well, while you contemplate, I must make haste. My brother will chair the meeting.' I was happy. I had always wanted to sit on the chair. I sat in Lordy's chair.

'One bastard gets up, and a real one sits down,' sneered Lordy.

'That is not a nice thing to say, as I felt it only fair I should speak in your defence.'

'I can speak in my defence,' he snarled.

'Very well then. I will prosecute.' Lordy looked at me, scornfully.

'You are a fool, and I have a degree in law. The priests broke the law by preaching prohibited religious dogma for which the penalty is death. This offence was committed on my estate. In my capacity as lord of this estate where the crime was perpetrated, I sentenced them to death and hung them. I broke no law. Therefore, I demand to be set free.' I banged the table.

'I would point out to the prisoner that he no longer holds that position, and the law now states the hanging was murder and the penalty, death.'

'When my army gets here and finds I have been harmed in any way, they will torch every house and kill every tenant.'

'This army you speak of, who will feed them?' I asked.

'They will bring their supplies.'

'And when they leave? How many men were billeted here?' I asked.

'A hundred. Maybe forty horses.'

'Where did Lordy get the food for them,' I asked.

'From us, instead of rent,' Faith answered.

'You have plenty for four thousand when they come. We have barely enough now,' Hope replied. 'Lord Stapleton was generous with our possessions, giving them all to you and turning us out as beggars. Perhaps he should show similar kindness now, giving all his remaining belongings also to his tenants.' I left the question hanging in the air.

'What?' says the jury. Their heads swivelled towards Faith, Hope and Charity, as did the cold eye of Lordy. There was a hurried consultation.

'He should be released,' their verdict.

'Very well,' I said. 'Lord Woodford will be back within days. You can release him to him. On the other hand, if he begs you to take back the grain and begs you to release him today, I think you should consider the request.' Lord Stapleton growled something under his breath.

'He wants to stay,' I said. 'I will lock him in the guard-house.'

He was clearer the next time.

'Take back your grain, and I wish to leave now. With your permission,' he added. I walked beside him to the gate, where James joined us. 'Enjoy your empty victory, Landers. When you leave here you will be gone forever, I will be back.'

Then, Lord Stapleton turned his back on us and walked away, with dignity.

THE PARTING

James led the way through the gates of Landers' Hall, Lordy's guests in two carts behind him, then Lordy's soldiers tied to the cart by a long rope. Wexford and I jostled for position in front of his men, who brought up the rear. When well clear of Landers' Hall, the prisoners were released. Wexford watched as his love left his life, his eyes anxious just before she disappeared. She raised her hand and gave a little wave. I leaned closer to see his face, and thought I saw a small tear, before dodging a backwards swipe of his paw.

'She reminded me of someone I used to know,' Wexford said sadly. 'You would not understand,' he finished in his usual snarl.

'We will go our separate ways now,' James announced. 'Most of you have families to go to, some have to call on the families of our lost friends. I will join O'Neill in the north; if you wish to rejoin, come in your own time.' Wexford agreed.

'We are safer to break up now. They may send a troop looking for a group.'

'I have to go back,' I announced. 'Back to my parish.'

James looked surprised.

'You have no friends back there now.'

'Maybe one,' I replied.

'He has to hump Moira Doherty,' Wexford said unhelpfully. I glared at him.

'You would not understand.' I threw back at him as I wheeled Sleepy and headed back. I kept to the forest, only breaking cover when I could progress no further. Then, through the trees, I could see my old church carefully skirting the village. I came to Doherty's house. From my hide, I watched her come with the basket. I waited until the food was eaten. When she left, I nudged Old Sleepy and overtook her. She looked up at me, startled.

'You should not be here,' she said. 'They are looking for you. It seems you are a bigger sinner than me.' Her face was flushed.

'We could have,' she began.

'I know,' I said. She smiled.

'We were like that.'

'I know,' I said.

'I can't leave them,' she said.

'I know,' I replied.

'You can't stay here,' she pointed out.

'I know,' I said. 'I have something for you,' I said. I took out a bag of coins. 'The war will not last forever. When it is safe, take your family and start a new life.' She took it, her eyes brimming. She took my hand and looked around.

'We could,' she began. She looked into my eyes. 'But we won't, will we?' She was puzzled.

'The next time you feel like this, let it, someone, with a future, a decent man who offers love and kindness, not food for your family or coins for your future.' I had been listening to the hoofbeats. They were getting closer.

'I must go,' I said. 'I wish.'

'I know,' she answered, smiling.

'Tell your sister it was the best I could do.' I left her, smiling and returned to the cover of the trees and watched as they passed by, led by a garishly dressed man who I knew to be Lord Ormond. He had been to Landers' Hall to visit my father in the days before his death. If a request for aid had been made, it was refused. Well now, I thought, it's yours for free. In the rear was Lord Woodford. The vultures were circling for Landers' Hall

THE HUNTED

I worked my way back to the woods above our cottage. Down below, I could see Ormond's men troop through the open gates; of Lord Stapleton and the tenants, there was no sign. I sent Sleepy into a trot as I watched the proceedings at the hall, keeping as far as possible from the great house. I had missed something. Lord Woodford had learned from his previous mistake. He was also watching from the trees, and had kept a guard of six around him. This I noticed when I heard a bellow of rage from the trees as I trotted past. Woodford was doing his dance of temper again, pointing at me and shouting 'kill him, get him.' I was in full gallop before his soldiers got the message I was to be stopped, killed, hung. They came after me. The first two drove their horses hard and began to gain. I urged Sleepy on, and the hoofbeats faded. I looked back, hoping the pursuit was over. The first two had eased down, and the second pair took up the chase. A feeling of unease came over me. These were a different type of soldier; they were working to a plan. I heard hoofbeats getting closer again. I asked Sleepy for more, and the hoofbeats faded. Then came the final two. Sleepy's neck was covered in sweat; bits of foam flew past me. I looked back; they had drifted away from each other to prevent any chance of my turning for cover. Sleepy's breath was getting ragged, and suddenly a cold temper took control of me. I eased him down. They were gaining now, still wide apart. Sleepy's breathing became less urgent. I stopped and turned him.

I drew my sword and drove Sleepy at his nearest pursuer. Sleepy was happier now; I felt him bunch his muscles as he approached the other horse, who shied sideways to avoid a collision, catching his rider off guard as I rammed the sword into his exposed right side. He clung to his horse for a few strides before toppling off. Before he hit the ground, we were heading for the second pursuer. When the other soldier saw Sleepy charging at him at full gallop, he decided to turn for home. It was a mistake. Sleepy crashed into the horse's side mid-turn, and horse and rider were upended. The rider was quickly on his feet and running, looking fearsomely over his shoulder; as he ran, we left him go. I reached over and patted Sleepy on the neck, and his teeth barely missed my returning hand.

'I will take that as a sign of affection,' I said. His blood was up. He turned his head, looked at me, rolled his eyes, and tried to bite my leg. I kicked him lightly on the nose; we were becoming friends. The sightless eyes of the fallen soldier seemed to follow me as I rode away. I had added murder to my list of sins.

DARKNESS

I became more cautious. I had not changed clothes, and still wore the stolen uniform likely to put me in further danger. I took to hiding by the day and travelling by night. Looking at the sun by day, I believed I was travelling north, but in truth, I was lost. I became increasingly worried I had added murder to my list of crimes. I tried to convince myself that it was not murder; it was an act of war. Then the thought came I had just killed a Catholic soldier wearing the wrong uniform. Not only did I need a priest, but I also needed a patient, very forgiving one, or forgiveness would be quickly followed by extreme unction. Sleepy, who had been plodding along through the darkness while I examined my conscience, came to halt, ears pricked. In the darkness ahead, I could see a flickering torch lighting up a large building. I could make out the outline of other houses. I found a ruined house where I left Sleepy and walked towards the buildings. It was quiet; I

85

reasoned it might be later than I thought. Against the night sky, I recognised the tall building as a church. I reached for the door; it would not open, but I could see a light flickering against a window. I moved around to the rear. I was reaching for the sacristy door when it opened, and a man came out holding a torch in one hand and a bag in the other.

'What do you want?' he asked; his voice was not friendly.

'I want to see the priest,' I said.

'Everyone wants to see the priest,' he said curtly. 'Well, hurry it up, then help Rodger at the front door. Then mount that over it.' Working on the church, I thought, but the priest was here. I took the bag and went inside through another door. I could see the altar; they had taken down the life-sized crucifix and laid it on the altar. Four candles burned around it.

'Father,' I called in a loud whisper. There was a smell of something familiar, candles maybe. No not candles.

'Father,' I called again. I began to wonder how I would begin to tell my terrible sins. The lights from the candle drew me to the altar. A waxen hand extended towards me. I reached to touch it. Blood, my brain said, the smell. I stood on something slippery and grabbed the hand to steady myself; it fell with me to the floor. I scrambled to my feet. A man had been spreadeagled on the altar, but the ropes that had held him were no longer of use, as the limbs had been cut from the body. My horrified eyes dropped to the waist; and below, I knew what I had slipped on. There was no head. I knew what was in the bag. I jumped away from the sight, my stomach emptying. As I gasped for breath, someone laughed.

'You must be new,' came a voice from the dark. 'I worked in a slaughterhouse before I came here.'

'You are Rodger,' I croaked. I needed time to think.

'And you?' he asked.

'John,' I answered.

'Jer went for some food; this is a big job.' I followed him towards the front door. There they were, the torch slowly revealing what my brain could not cope with. The fog cleared from my head and I knew what had happened here. The town had been besieged; the men on the walls. The women and children had gone where they felt safest – their church. They were still here. Mothers, children and babies in a mass of blood and severed limbs. The front door had held, but not the back.

'Forget the children,' Rodger said.

'What?' I asked; my voice seemed to come from a long way off.

'The children rarely have valuables. Just the women. Here. I will show you.' He grabbed a leg. You could see through the blood and gore that she had dressed well. He pulled her undergarments and looked into her orifices.

'The women are clever. They hide things,' he said by way of explanation. 'No, nothing there.' He dropped the leg. 'Ring on her finger though.' He picked up the lifeless hand. 'We will have to cut it off; they swell, you know.' He spoke as a teacher to a dim-witted pupil. I drew my sword.

'For feck sake,' he said. 'Have you nothing smaller?' I brought the sword down; the shock of it striking ran up my arm, again and again, until Rodger was at one with his work. I was walking back towards the altar when Jer came back.

'The rest of the crew have pulled out,' Jer said. 'Where is Rodger?'

'Gone,' I said. 'Did we have too? I asked.

'What?' Jer looked at me.

'Rob the dead,' I finished.

'That's what armies do, boy,' he replied. 'How do you think we get paid?

'One last job, Jer,' announced the head over the door. I handed him the sack. He reached inside and brought out the head, turning it towards himself.

'For a dead priest, he does not look very happy,' he concluded. 'Hold this,' he ordered, 'while I get something to mount it on,' thrusting the head into my hands. He returned with a long pole used to extinguish candles.

'Hold this,' he handed me the pole. I gave him the head and lowered the pole to waist high. As he prepared to stick the head to the steel snuffer, I rammed it into his stomach, pinning him against the wall.

'It will be your head,' I told him as his eyes followed my sword to his neck as I began to hack. I retrieved the priest's head and brought it to the altar. I put everything in place. I found some altar cloths and covered him up to his neck. He looked almost normal. I was tired. I sat in the pew in front of him. I told him my sins without speaking. He forgave me. I told him I would confess to him any future sins I might commit. I had found the only priest that would forgive me – a dead one.

I heard him coming, but did not look around. He sat at the end of the pew. I could feel his eyes on me.

'Were you here?' he asked. 'Were you here when they killed them.'

'No,' I said. 'I was not here. I tried to stop them. I ordered my dragoons to stand between the women and the children and those madmen. They wanted the priest; we gave them the priest.' His haunted eyes swung towards the altar. 'When they finished with the priest. They sent for the commander, Cromwell himself. We pleaded for mercy for the women and children. Cromwell ordered us to stand down, or our actions would be regarded as mutiny. He said the message must go out to all Royalists and Irish that resistance means death. We stood down. The black-clad madmen butchered them in front of our eyes. One quoted from the Bible as he swung a child's head against the wall.'

'I am just a soldier. Does that excuse me?' he asked. He was not talking to me; he was looking at the innocents dead in the annexe. He sighed.

'Well, duty calls. I am on lookout in the belfry. We hold the centre of the town; not enough men to man the walls. You should go there. We are expecting trouble from survivors.' He climbed the stairs to the belfry. I looked down at the uniform that I had worn since Landers' Hall. Stiff with blood. I wanted it off. I searched the houses around the church. In one, I found clothes to fit. As I emerged from the house to leave, he called down from the belfry.

'I don't blame you. I wish I had the courage to desert. Good luck.' I walked back to Sleepy. The dawn was breaking as we passed a milestone. It said: 'Welcome to Drogheda'.

There was no need to hide now. I was just another traveller on the road seeking directions. I noticed the pitiful state of those that I met; their supplies of food taken by those responsible for seeing their soldiers were fed. It was clear to me that many would not survive the winter. I soon learned to avert my eyes from their plight; a further sign of life descending into darkness. The town was a welcome sight, full of ordinary people going about their business. I found a stable for Sleepy, paid the steep price charged for hay and grain, and took myself to an eating house. Many rich-looking couples sat eating, and some of them looked up with raised eyebrows as I entered. I became aware I had brought the smell of horse sweat with me. Undeterred, I wiped my hands on the seat of my pants and sat down. A man who served at table approached. He seemed to be looking at the ceiling and me at the same time.

'Sir,' he said, 'you might have entered the wrong establishment.' I looked around; those that were not watching were eating.

'Food,' I said.

'Sir,' he began. I looked into his eyes and everything that I had seen and become went into my next word.

'Food.' He stepped back like I had pushed him. He took a slate from under his arm and handed it to me. I looked at it. There were very few familiar words on it, but when I looked at the prices, I realised he might have been trying to save me embarrassment. I softened towards him, and whispered.

'Which has the most on the plate?' He bent towards me, brushed a crumb of the table and whispered back.

'The mutton, sir.'

'I will have that,' I said thankfully, putting my hand in my pocket and holding out the price of the meal. He gently pushed my hand aside.

'Later. Sir, later will be fine.' He glided into the kitchen. After a considerable time had elapsed, he reappeared and placed a platter on the table in front of me covered by a dome which he removed with a flourish. I looked at it open-mouthed. A small round piece of mutton sat in the middle of a large plate, surrounded by a line of gravy in the shape of a sheep, surrounded in turn by a round of lettuce leaves. With much ado, he produced one large potato that had burst its skin with the heat and left it beside it. I looked at him, thinking maybe it was a joke. He was gazing at the ceiling again.

'Will that be all, sir?' he asked.

'What more could anyone want?' I said, sarcasm dripping from my voice.

'Indeed, sir,' he replied, and minced off. The meal had only awakened the hunger in my stomach, which growled in protest as I paid and made my way onto the street, where I beheld much drunkenness and lewd behaviour. I saw a sign 'ale and bed' that described what I was looking for, and went in. The customers looked different from the ones in the eating house. I had gone from one extreme to another. I approached the large plank behind which a fat woman with an ample bosom, most of which was exposed, leaned towards me, putting under threat the small bits of modesty which were retained by her dirty beerstained blouse.

'Ale,' I said, 'and a bed.' She filled a jug of ale from a barrel behind her and slapped it down before me. I picked it up, the jug, and had a big slug from it.

'Are you forgetting something?' she asked.

'Thanks,' I said; her eyes narrowed unpleasantly.

'Sam,' she called out in a loud voice. A massive brute of a fellow smelling of beer and piss appeared at my elbow.

'What's the matter, love?' he asked the woman, but never taking his eyes of me.

'He has not paid,' she said.

'I want a bed also,' I said.

'I suppose you would like my wife in it too,' he asked. I had another look at her and hastily declined.

'Just the bed.'

'Why? What's wrong with her?' he asked.

'Why, nothing,' I said, trying desperately to follow what was happening. 'I want a jug of ale and a bed for the night.' I began to think maybe you paid first in this establishment.

'I will pay now,' I offered, taking out some coins. 'That for the ale, that for the bed.' I laid them on the plank.

'What about my wife?' he asked. 'Do you want her for nothing?'

'No,' I said to calm him, 'I would not take her for anything.'

'You wouldn't take her for anything?' he echoed, his face getting redder. I thought he was going to attack me, and backed off when someone in the gloom of the alehouse burst out laughing. I heard a familiar voice I hated saying, 'Leave him, Sam,' and Sam, whose face was reddening with suppressed laughter, burst out. Wexford, who had been drinking with Sam when I came in, slapped me on the back.

'Now buy some ale and pay like everybody else.' I did so, but I hated him even more than before, if indeed that was possible.

O'NEILL

The sun woke me. I opened my eyes. The glare of its rays sent shooting pains through my head. I turned away from the sun. My brains rattled painfully against my skull. The memories came – Drogheda, Wexford, ale, bed. My feet were on the pillow beside me. It took me some moments to conclude that my head and my feet could not be on the pillow at the same time. I rose my head gingerly. Wexford's ugly head was lying beside my feet at the bottom of the bed. The sight was too much for my stomach. I leaned over the side of the bed and added to the already half-full chamber pot. Not mine, I questioned, but then I saw the lettuce. I lay back and was drifting into a fitful sleep when Wexford slapped me awake.

'Food,' he said. The food was served by Sam's wife, who looked no better than the night before. She slapped hairy bacon and runny eggs in front of us both. My stomach contracted again, but it had given all.

'Not eating?' Wexford noted, scooping the contents of my plate into his. 'You must have eaten something that did not agree with you,' he observed, as his tongue pursued the egg yolk down his chin. My stomach heaved again. I left him there. I had wanted to tell him about Drogheda. Each time I tried, my mind questioned the facts. Was it a nightmare? I hoped it was, and feared that voicing it would make it real. But I looked at the clothes I wore, and tried to remember where I got them. The street was full of men who seemed to be going in one direction. A fellow fell into step beside me; he was young and full of excitement.

'The priest said we would be fed and paid as well,' he said. 'Is that true?'

'For what?' I enquired. He was joining O'Neill's army.

'Is that not where you are going?' he questioned. O'Neill's army. Those words struck a chord –our meeting place. We turned a corner, and there were two queues.

'Army or appointment?' I was asked. I was about to say 'army' when I saw James.

'Appointment,' I said, and ran to his side just as his name was called. We entered the courtyard, and seated at a table surrounded by armed men was Owen Roe O'Neill. We were at the rear of a long line of people. The first in the queue was a landowner complaining about the amount of food demanded from him to feed the army. Feed it well, for if this army is defeated you will have no land on which to grow it. Next was a man in uniform who announced himself as Captain Blount, seeking urgent help to lift a siege in a town called Drogheda. Drogheda – the name forced my mind to confront the darkness it contained.

'Nothing lives in that place,' I said, as much to myself as to anyone else. All around me heard. 'Arrest them,' came a shout from a group of clerics who had been conducting a service at the side of the courtyard. With a sinking heart, I recognised the voice of Bishop Watkins, as Captain Blount caught me by the throat.

'What did you say?' he cried.

'Nothing lives within the walls of Drogheda; not priest, not man, not woman, not a child,' I said, as armed soldiers descended on us. He began to shake me.

'I have a wife and children there. You are lying,' he pleaded.

'I sat with them for a while,' I said, as the tears in my eyes told him it was true.

'You have charges to lay against these men?' O'Neill asked the bishops. The bishop was about to list them when O'Neill interrupted him.

'They will be placed under guard. I will hear your charges tomorrow.' James and I were taken to a gated compound and thrown inside. I looked around. We were surrounded by the dregs of the earth.

'Two more for the rope tomorrow,' said one guard to the other as he turned the key. After a few hours, they were joined by another with a jar of whiskey. Raucous laughter ensued, broken only by the need to take their turn drinking. Then all fell silent. I could hear keys rattling at the door, but the door did not open. Curious, I walked closer and looked through a crack in the door. Wexford was at the door, fumbling with the keys.

'What are you doing,' I said.

'Trying to get out,' he said and hiccupped.

'Well, open the door,' I said, 'and you will be out.'

'How,' he said, 'do I open the door?'

'With the key,' I replied, trying to restrain myself from abusive comments.

'I know that,' he answered belligerently. 'Do you think I am stupid?' He fell against the door, banging his head.

'Wexford,' I said patiently, 'put the key in the keyhole and turn it.'

'Which one?' he asked.

'Hold the keys up so I can see them through the crack,' I suggested, grinding my teeth in frustration. The keys waved back and forwards in front of the crack.

'Wexford,' I said as patiently as possible, 'there are only two keys on that ring and they both look the same.'

'I know that,' he slurred. 'Do you think I am stupid?' I bit my tongue.

'Of course not.'

I decided to start again.

'Wexford, put the key in the keyhole and turn it.'

'Sure das my problem all along,' he hiccupped again. 'Which keyhole? I resigned myself to being hung, but then a flash of inspiration hit me.

'The one in the middle,' I concluded. There was a scrape of a key in the lock, and the door opened. 'Why did you not tell me that sooner?' he demanded. Then he belched and fell at my feet. I looked furtively around. James was at the far side of the compound surrounded by the unsavoury cellmates. I closed out the door quietly, dragged Wexford against the wall, and put him in a sitting position. I caught James' eye and beckoned; I showed him the keys. Wexford was snoring, a dribble hanging out of the corner of his mouth.

'We can't leave him,' I said surprising myself.

'We will collect him later,' James assured me. When we were unobserved by the others, we slipped quietly out, throwing the keys on top of the sleeping guards. I followed as James walked towards the courtyard. There was a different man at the gate.

'Landers,' James said. 'We are on the list.'

'Yes, you are listed go on in.'

O'Neill still sat at the table. Gathered around him looking at a map were some officers, Captain Blount amongst them. They looked up in various levels of surprise as James announced himself 'Landers of Landers' Hall'.

'What brings you back here?' O'Neill asked. 'I have heard the charges against you.'

'Then you know we have nowhere else to go,' James replied. Owen Roe O'Neill looked at James with a curious expression.

'We have here a man who engaged two superior forces and came away with a ransom, released himself from jail and now confronts the man who put him there. Such a man deserves to be heard.' James had the floor.

'The savagery of Drogheda will open many gates for the Parliament. The barriers that stay shut must be strengthened to give you time to gather your forces to confront them.'

'What do you propose?' O'Neill seemed mildly amused.

'Put me in command of one hundred men along with my own. We will harry them as they move south and delay them at every turn.'

'Who in my army would follow you?' O'Neill asked.

'Captain Blount,' James suggested, 'as we will make our first engagement Drogheda.'

'Captain Blount?' O'Neill's eyes swung towards the captain.

'Yes,' Captain Blount agreed, 'but I will be in command.'

'We will talk in the morning,' O'Neill said. The next morning, we were summoned to O'Neill's chamber. The light from the window showed a bearded face, brown parchment skin stretched over protruding bones. The darkness of the night before had been kinder.

'My position here is not a good one. I have approached the Parliament for terms, and the Royalists. I trust neither. The Parliament invading my country means I must side with the Royalists under pressure from the church. My fear is when they settle their differences, they will come for me, and this land of ours and our faith and way of life will be no more. Be in the courtyard at noon for your trial. Now I must prepare a reason for your release for my papal benefactors.'

'And the other prisoners,' prompted James.

'That I cannot do. They are already condemned to hang at noon.'

We waited in the courtyard for our trial. Like the day before, they queued to give support or to ask help; one of which was a priest called Fr Casey from a place called Clonmel who, further frightened by the news of the faith of Drogheda, sought help, as the Royalist commander had vowed before God to defend the town to the death.

'I have here in this courtyard a man that will carry my name to Clonmel, with a further force to follow.'

'Landers of Landers' Hall,' the clerk called out. 'What are the charges against those men?' Bishop Watkins was on his feet. He must have been up all night, so great was his list.

'Guilty or not guilty?' asked O'Neill.

'Guilty,' James said. O'Neill banged the table.

'It is the sentence of this court that the Landers brothers go from here to a place called Clonmel to defend it with honour.' The bishop was on his feet.

'They have no honour. They will flee.'

'Do you wish to go with them to ensure they do not?' O'Neill enquired. The bishop sat down.

'Do you accept the sentence?' O'Neill asked.

'We will carry your name to Clonmel and defend it with honour,' James agreed. Captain Blount was waiting with his troop. Sleepy was sniffing a mare as I approached, and gave me a mean eye. I grabbed him and threw on the saddle. I was getting used to avoiding his teeth. I tightened his girth and swung aboard. There was a church behind the courtyard I had not noticed before. Going in the door was the Clonmel priest Fr Casey and Bishop Watkins. To pray for our expedition, I hoped. I rejoined James and Captain

Blount. I noticed about twenty of our old crew had also appeared.

'You understand I am in command?' Blount confronted James.

'Of course, Captain,' James agreed. Captain Blount led out, while James hung back near the cart carrying provisions as we neared the jail.

'Hold,' he called. Captain Blount pulled up.

'I see no shovels,' James said.

'What do you want shovels for?' Captain Blount asked.

'To bury the hanged men,' James said. 'O'Neill wants us to bury them away from the compound.' 'We are hanging them at noon,' the jailer said.

'I will not wait that long,' Captain Blount announced.

'Right,' said James. 'Give the shovels to those two.' I unloaded the shovels.

'They only need two,' I pointed out.

'Give them an extra one. They have a lot of digging to do.' The guards exchanged glances; this did not seem to their liking.

'There is another way,' said James. 'Get them out.' I went to the door. As it opened, Wexford saw me and went for me. I ducked behind a guard who used a cosh to subdue him.

'Line them up,' James ordered. He produced a rope from the cart ordered the guard to tie them. Then James stuck a shovel through the ropes of every second one.

'Now,' he told the guards, 'we will march them to a grove of trees. Get them to dig the holes, then we will hang them.'

'Times like this, you can see why they give the orders,' I overheard one jailer say to the other as we went on our way. James rode up to Captain Blount.

'I am sure you want to proceed to Drogheda to ensure no supplies get into the town. We will do what has to be done and join you later.'

'Yes,' Blount said. 'Your men appear to be more suited for that sort of work.' wheeled his horse and led his men away at a gallop. I went to Wexford, who had been eying me malevolently. I thought it best to leave him tied up until I explained what had happened. He confessed it was his fault, as Sam had given him a powder to knock out the guards; but as they drank, nothing seemed to be happening; and they were having such a good time, he joined them.

'What about them?' I asked, indicating the other prisoners.

'Pirates,' Wexford said. 'The scourge of the sea. Shipwrecked of the coast. They stare at you; if they have a leader, he keeps to himself.' I looked along the line of pirates; few ordinary people would like to be in their company. They made Wexford and his men look respectable in comparison. We had reached a line of trees. James dismounted and called a halt. He walked along the line of pirates, staring at each in turn.

'You have chosen not to talk to me, so it falls on me to speak to you. As it stands, you are no use to me alive.' He was observing them. 'So I should carry out the sentence and hang ye. However, you are no use to me dead either. I have decided to set you free. Ye can leave here unarmed in a strange country, or you can follow me. I intend to do on land as you did on the sea. Ye shall share such riches or misfortune that befall us. If you take this course, you will obey my orders without question. Anyone who takes arms from me and deserts me I will hang.' His words hung in the air as he looked from one to the other. He stepped forwards; long greasy hair, crazy staring eyes.

'I will accept your articles, except one. I will carry arms with you, but if any of my men have to hang, I will do it,' he said. His name was Garcia. We called him greasy; it seemed to suit him.

RETURN TO DROGHEDA

James' plan was simple; we watched the roads into Drogheda at a distance. They were under siege. They did not know that. First, they came out in small groups, and if insight of the town were allowed to return. As they needed to travel further to graze their horses and purchase supplies for themselves, we struck. Blount and his men fell on them with a ferocity that in turn made James furious, as he wanted prisoners.

'Prisoners,' he shouted. 'Prisoners. Do you know what that means? People that can talk. I need to know things.' But at least we had more horses than we needed, and we went further afield and traded them for food. Then, James got the idea of loading it on our cart. I sat beside him as we drove it to Drogheda. We went in the same way I had a week earlier. The sentry on the church belfry called us to halt and gave the bell a thug. Four soldiers walked up the street.

'What do you want?' a surly Sergeant asked.

'We were told we would be paid well for supplies,' James said in a wheedling voice.

'And who told you that?'

'Soldiers we met yesterday,' James said.

'They did not come back last night,' said the Sergeant.

'Well, we did sell them some whiskey,' said James, 'and they were asking about women.'

'They will be sorry when they come back,' he said. 'But we do need supplies.'

The sergeant pulled out a purse counted coins into James' hand.

'You can have a bushel of oats and a bag of potatoes for that,' said James.

'I want it all,' said the Sergeant in a very mean tone.

'Then I suggest you pay me for it.'

'I could take it,' said the Sergeant nodding to his men.

'I am told milord Cromwell hung some men for stealing from ordinary people like us,' said James. 'Perhaps he wants to make amends for what happened here,' he added.

'Alright, follow me,' he said. 'I will get your money, you robber.' I struck by the way he took offence to being overcharged after killing and robbing the whole town. We drove behind him on turning into the street; from where they had come, we saw them, or what was left of them. They had been burned. Nothing left but bones in a great pile of ashes. However, the stench of death still hung in the air, and I knew why the robbers of the dead had been in such a hurry. We stopped the cart outside a building while the sergeant went in and reappeared with our money. We drove a little further and unloaded. The sergeant was studying us, and I began to feel uneasy. He walked over to us.

'I will pay extra if ye clear the street.' He indicated the huge pile of bones and ashes. I began to retch with the thought. James haggled until a price was agreed. We spent the day hauling cartful after cartful of bones to the river. In the course of the day, I met the soldier who had spoken to me in the chapel. He complimented me quietly on my change of occupations. He said he wished he could do the same, as his nights were sleepless and tormented.

We left in good terms, with the promise of further supplies within days. James and I called on Captain Blount, who was in charge of the west side of Drogheda. James had thought it best to keep the parties separate, as Blount was not aware of our recruits. I followed James to Blount's camp; he called the troops together to outline his plan for Drogheda. When James said we had gone into Drogheda, Blount asked why.

'I needed to know their strength; required to see the layout of their defences. Tomorrow we will attack them. You will lead your men into the town from the west. The outskirts are not defended. You will encounter a lookout post. Discharge your weapons. They may send men to engage you. Do not enter the town centre. My men will attack from the east. When you hear our assault, you will fall back and skirt the town and come to our aid. They will follow us out and be caught in the open. Do not follow them into the town.'

'Ye were in the town,' Captain Blount accused. 'Tell me' he said 'what you found there.'

'Ashes,' James said. 'All reduced to ashes.'

'What happened there?' Blount persisted.

'Why you asking now?' James enquired.

'Because you smell of death,' he said.

'They burned the bodies. The bones are in the river. We helped.'

'Why?' he shouted.

'Because I needed to know their strength and the lay-out of their defences,' said James quietly, 'and you killed those that might tell me. Now sit and listen.' And we went through it over and over again.

LEAVING DROGHEDA

The next day, we were back in Drogheda. The man on the belfry rang the bell to announce our presence. We pulled in against the church wall to wait, as Greasy slipped out from under the cart and into the church. The sergeant and two dragoons led us into the centre as before, and we unloaded as before. The sergeant went into his office to pay us. Then Blount attacked from the west. A thunder of hoofs, then musket and pistol shots. The sergeant came out on the run, shouting for his men to take their positions. James and I ran in where he had come out. Three dragoons were manning the windows, their muskets at the ready.

'Where are ye going?' asked one.

'Dangerous out there,' said James, as the sounds of shots and screams came from west got louder. A door was open leading into a back room. I wandered over and looked through it. It was all there – coins, rings, gold teeth, crosses, chalices. Three more dragoons guarded the rear windows. I went, 'god all mighty,' in a loud voice as I picked up a large cross in one hand, a chalice in the other. 'This reminds me of when I was a priest.' James walked in the door behind me and said, 'Me too', as he closed the door behind him and began to chant in Latin. They turned, looking at us, mouths open.

'Just a jest,' I said. 'Just a joke.'

'Put that gold down and get out of here,' said one, 'or we will do you up like a priest, you Irish Catholic pig.' That was his lot. As silent as the rats in their ship, they were in the windows, Greasy and his men; knives plunged and slashed. James and I loaded loot into sacks, passing them out as more hands appeared at the windows. James opened the door, and we walked out to the other room. The shots and shouting were growing distant.

'Looks like we can go now,' said James.

'Yes. Looks that way,' agreed one of the soldiers. We strolled out the door, got in our cart and trotted up the street. Greasy and his men piled on the loot. We were not gone far when the shouting started. The three dragoons were out in the street shouting for the sergeant, who was soon running up the street after us with a large body of dragoons. We passed the church where the bell ringer was staring at us with lifeless eyes.

'Sleep well, my friend,' I said. Outside the town was the hovel where I had left Sleepy on my first visit to Drogheda. There, we jumped off the cart and took cover with the rest of our men, who silently handed us loaded muskets and pistols. The sergeant and around forty dragoons had passed the church. They saw us jump from the cart to the hovel. He may have wondered why, but the need to get his loot back outweighed any caution. We rose as one and discharged our muskets into them. They returned fire and kept coming. They were in the open with spent weapons, when Blount's cavalry hit them. The sergeant lost interest in the loot and shouted at his men to retreat to the town. Blount and his Drogheda troop cut into them with bloodthirsty relish. The sergeant had gathered his men. They became a tightly packed unit retreating towards the town, as Blount's cavalry circled them. They reached the town. James said, 'That should keep them.' He shouted and waved at Blount to break off. Blount looked at James and looked at the town, and charged in past the church. His men followed. James ran around in circles with temper. A volley of shots was heard from the town. Blount reappeared, but six riderless horses followed. Blount was happy. He rode up to James.

'What happened?' asked James.

'They ran before us like sheep,' he said.

'What happened this time?' James asked a soldier behind Blount who was sitting with head bowed.

'We followed them like sheep, right into the centre of town. There must have been a musket in every window and door. We lost six men, four wounded; if they had waited for us to go further in, none of us would have got out.' James looked at Blount.

'Have you anything to say?'

'We are at war,' said Blount. 'We killed three times that number. That's what matters.'

'No,' James said. 'What matters is the death of seven men because you did not follow orders. Pistol.' I handed him mine. He shot Blount between the puzzled eyebrows. James looked at the shocked faces around him.

'He had no value on your life. We already had what we came here for,' James said, pointing to the cart. 'A share for every man who follows me.' There was silence for a while, then the one which James had asked about Blount's charge asked, 'What now?'

'Well, in there,' he pointed to Drogheda, 'they now know our strength. In an hour, maybe less, they will come out like wasps out of a disturbed nest. We will not be here. We are going to run.'

ORMOND

We made our way south, sending scouts in all directions to avoid confrontation from any side. It was on one of these missions that I crested a rise and, camped below me, were the butchers of Drogheda – Cromwell's Model Army. I was looking at an army of thousands of men and hundreds of horses. I knew fear – this was the army we had sworn to confront in a town called Clonmel. I returned in haste to inform James. He called us together.

'Just as Lordy said, they would take the coastal towns to ensure supplies. In front of them, a few strongholds that may or may not offer resistance.' Then James looked at Wexford. 'Wexford town'. We gave Cromwell's army a wide berth. Within hours, we came across another command. A green flag and harp fluttered on a pole as James, Wexford and I rode in.

'Who leads this army?' James asked the sentry who confronted us.

'The Earl of Ormond,' was the reply.

'Take me to him,' James ordered.

'Who shall I announce?' the sentry asked.

'Landers,' James said. 'of Landers' Hall.'

'Wait here,' the sentry said. 'I doubt he will see you. He is a busy man.' He returned looking surprised. 'He will see you.' We followed him to a tent at the centre of the camp which contained the Earl of Ormond. Resplendent and pompous, he surveyed us as we entered. He viewed James up and down.

'You are James Landers? How disappointing. I was expecting a large man, possibly with horns. But then the bishop tends to be dramatic. Does he not? He would have me detain you were he here. However, I am kindly disposed towards you. Your actions have delivered Landers' Hall to me, which I believe was planned as an enemy stronghold.'

'I am here to offer a further service,' James replied. 'We have undertaken to defend a town, and any effort to weaken our foes would benefit our cause. We have stolen their food taken their horses. But now their escorts are too strong. We need more men to disrupt their supply. With five hundred men I could ensure hunger would prevail in Cromwell's army.'

'You expect me to ask my soldiers to take orders from a leader who is nothing more than a common thief?' I looked at Wexford, and we both looked at James. James left the snub pass.

'I need not lead them. I would suggest yourself take five hundred men, and you would be in their camp in two hours. Sweep in and drive off their horses. That would destroy their nights' sleep and delay their progress south.'

'Two hours?' Ormond had picked up on the time.

'Yes,' said James. We passed their camp last night.

'Then I must waste no more time with you. I must consult with real soldiers.' We were left standing in the tent. Wexford shrugged and picked up a chicken leg from Ormond's half-eaten dinner.

'Fool?' he questioned.

'Coward,' I suggested.

'Both,' said James, 'but smart enough to know it.'

WEXFORD TOWN

From across the grey water of the Slaney, we viewed the town of Wexford. I nudged Wexford. 'You are home.'

'Yes,' he said. 'Home'. He sounded timid; not the Wexford I knew and disliked. He turned his horse towards the ferry.

'Go with him,' James said. 'He might need a friend.'

'A friend?' I echoed. 'Well, someone in there might remember him as a baby,' I concluded.

'Go with him,' James repeated; this time it was an order. I joined Wexford on the ferry. Sleepy did not like it, nor for that matter did I. I gazed into the murky depths of the Slaney.

'You were used to this,' I challenged Wexford as he gazed thoughtfully at the approaching town. He ignored me, so I switched my nervous attention to the ferryman.

'What if the rope broke?' I asked.

'Well, if the tide was coming in, not so bad. Out, not so good.'

'Which way is it going now?' I asked.

'Out,' he answered. We docked, and fear of drowning vanished; likewise the hunted feeling that I never knew I had until it was gone. The murky river between me and the warring factors removing that fear. I felt like a child at Christmas as I followed Wexford into the town. He turned down a side street and stopped at a house. His shoulders slumped as he studied the door. He dismounted and went to the door. He raised his hand to knock and left it down again. I dismounted.

'Did your family live here?' I asked. He nodded.

'Well, we must see are they still here,' I said, giving the door a repeated hard knock. A child around ten years old opened the door.

'Who is there, pet?' came a woman's voice from the house.

'Two men,' the child called back.

'Tell them to come in,' the woman called. 'I am putting bread into the oven.'

'Your parents must not live here anymore,' I suggested. Wexford looked at me blankly. Just then, a woman came through the door from the kitchen. She stopped in the doorway, looking at us. The dark-haired woman at Lordy's could have been her sister, except bitterness had taken the softness from her face.

'You?' she said, her eyes locked on Wexford. 'You?' she seemed lost for words. Then they came. 'You thieving drunken whoring lump of no good shit. You godless bas-

116

tard. Take that other scoundrel with you and get out of my house.' My mouth had dropped open. I said, 'That's a bit harsh.'

'Harsh?' she said. 'Harsh?' She seemed stuck for words again, before she found them. Wexford said quietly, 'Wives are like that.'

My mouth dropped open again.

'Wife?' she said. 'What would you know about wives, unless they were someone else's? Were you with one of your whores when your son was born?'

'Son?' I exclaimed, looking around, but the boy was gone.

'Son?' said Wexford, something strange lighting up his face. 'I have a son, Marg?'

'Yes, you have a son,' she seemed deflated. The fight was gone from her. 'I called him after you,' she said. 'Cyril'.

'Cyril,' I echoed. Then Cyril the son was back.

'That's them, father, they were frightening mother.' Behind the child, the one he had called father was a well-dressed handsome man fondling a pistol. Two others flanked him.

'Play with your friends, Cyril,' Marg said. The child ran off.

'You look like you have seen a ghost, Doyle,' Wexford said, 'and you took care of Marg just like you promised; and my son calling you father, should I thank you?' Wexford asked.

'When did he say he would take care of me?' asked Marg.

'The night I left, Marg.'

'The night you stole the money from father and left with one of Mammies girls,' hissed Marg. 'Is that what they told you, Marg?' asked Wexford. 'The girl left on a ship with a sailor. I had a different send-off, Doyle. He told me he would take care of you as he kicked in my teeth, broke a few ribs. I rolled into the water to get away from the beating. They shot me. I lived on that quay as a child. There was a place to shelter under it. When they were gone, I released a boat and let it drift. Some fishermen saw the boat and pulled me aboard. I tried to die, Marg, but the devil did not want me either.'

'Why did you leave it so long to return?'

'No point, Marg. Between kicks, Doyle told me your father ordered my death.'

'He would never do that,' Marg exclaimed.

'Why not ask him,' Wexford suggested.

'He is dead,' Marg announced.

'Natural causes was it, Marg?' Wexford's hand was on his pistol.

'No,' she answered. 'He was shot.' I backed away, hand on pistol; the hunted feeling was back. 'You own it all then, Marg,' Wexford said, 'and Doyle owns you.'

'No one owns me,' she snarled. Wexford smiled.

'You sound like the woman I married. But the facts are, Marg, Doyle is now number one in the business. He was number three when I went in the sea. That made number two your father; shot put him number one.'

'The business is mine,' Marg said. 'Joseph runs it for me.'

'Well, Marg, you tell Joseph to run along. I am back, and he is number three again.'

'Please, Joseph,' Marg said. 'I want no trouble.'

'Yes, run along Joseph,' Wexford mimicked in that mocking voice I hated. Doyle did not like it either. He looked from Wexford to Marg and back to Wexford.

'Tonight on the quay, pistols,' Doyle challenged.

'Just the two of us this time?' questioned Wexford.

'Just us two,' agreed Doyle. He beckoned his men, and they were gone.

We left Marg to gather her thoughts and proceeded into town. Wexford stopped at a hostelry with a sign 'Dalton' over the door. Leaving the horses in stables at the back, we went in. Business was good, twenty to thirty men in various stages of drunkenness sat around tables, while a few more leaned against the bar served by a bald barman wearing an apron.

'Who owns this place now?' asked Wexford. 'I hear old man Dalton is dead.'

'His daughter, Margaret. Mr Doyle runs it for her. He is not here now; he just left with his son.' 'I want a room,' Wexford said. 'Number ten. The one with a bath.'

'Sorry, Sir. We are full. Besides, Mr Doyle stays in number ten, and I can't give you that.'

'You don't have to,' said Wexford, stepping around him and taking the key that hung on the hook marked ten. 'Mr Doyle will understand,' said Wexford, handing him a coin. 'Send up hot water and a razor.'

'You don't believe in avoiding confrontation,' I said.

'I tried that once, right here in this town. I let Doyle get too big for his boots.' A boy came with a bucket of steaming water.

'You can go second,' Wexford said. I looked him up and down and concluded I would wait for fresh water. While Wexford went for his bath, I purchased a mug of beer, and it disappeared in a flash. I purchased another and another. Soon, I was in a relaxed state, and began to reflect on the route my life was taking, and quickly realised I needed something stronger than beer. I was looking at the jars on the shelves behind the bar when he tugged at my elbow. I looked down into two bloodshot eyes.

'Rum,' he said. 'Rum'. He had been watching me, studying the jars.

'Rum,' I said to the bald barman.

'For two,' suggested the bleary-eyed one, who was so much in need that he was licking his lips with the thought that I might agree.

'For two,' I said. He didn't wait for the barman to leave it down. He grabbed the mug, and it was gone. I raised mine and drank. I liked it. I could feel the heat rising from my toes up.

'I told you,' he said. He was licking his lips again.

'Two more,' I said grandly. He was slower this time. He was eying me up.

'I saw you coming in with Cyril.'

'Shush,' I said. 'We call him Wexford. Cyril's a secret.' He looked puzzled.

'No secrets between me and Cyril,' he said. 'We worked this town together.'

'Worked,' I said, 'is not a word I would use for what Cyril does.' He cackled and sipped his rum. Then he continued.

'Cyril was second in command to Dalton. Nothing happened in this town without us getting a part of it. Then Cyril took up with Dalton's daughter. Dalton didn't like that. He had bigger things in mind for her. No surprise to me when Cyril disappeared. Doyle kept saying to Dalton Cyril wanted everything, but it was Doyle wanted everything. Dalton was found dead in an alley later, and whose elbow was Marge holding at his funeral? Would you have a coin?' he asked; he was licking his lips again. I gave him one. He went to turn away, but stopped.

'I was not always a bum.' He paused. 'Stay away from Cyril. He's a dead man. Then maybe we all are. Cromwell's coming, and there's those around here that thinks the sun shines out of the king's arse. God help us all,' he said and was gone.

'Rum,' I said, because I now needed it. I looked in the mirror behind the bar and saw a gaunt, unshaven tousled-haired tramp. My head bowed in disbelief. I lifted it again, and in the mirror, I saw a richly clad gentleman with shiny skin and slicked-back hair. I smiled at myself. 'That's better,' I said aloud.

'You think so?' said Wexford. I refocused on the mirror and realised the gent was Wexford who stood beside me, looking at me critically.

'Your drunk,' he said, 'and you smell. More hot water, barman,' he ordered. I took a step towards the stairs, one foot got caught in the other. I remember Wexford grabbing me before the lights went out. When I woke up, I was in the bath with all my clothes on, and my head was throbbing. The bath was divided from the room by a curtain. I stripped off my clothes and relaxed in the warm water, the curtain opened. Wexford threw in a suit of clothes like I had never seen.

'Doyle has good taste in clothes,' he said. 'Put them on. I can't be walking around my town with you looking like a tramp.' I did so and off we went.

'Now,' said Wexford, 'let us see which of my friends remembers me.' We turned into a shop. A middle-aged man was fitting shoes on a man who was fussing about fit and appearance.

'I would like some shoes, Willie,' Wexford said quietly.

'I will be with you when I finish with this gentleman.

'Now, Willie,' Willie looked up, annoyed; then his expression changed.

'Sorry, sir, I didn't recognise you.' He jumped up and began handing us shoes to try on. The man he had been serving jumped up to protest, but when Willie said they are with Mr Doyle, he apologised and quickly left. Barbers next. Again, we were given swift attention. Back on the street smelling of rosewater, it was time to eat. After the best meal I ever had, Wexford leaned back on his chair.

'god,' he said. 'Its good to be home.' He saw me looking around with a hunted expression and said, 'Don't worry. The Doyles and the Cyrils of this world settle their differences at night.' He led me through a couple of alleys.

'There,' he said. 'There it is, the waterfront. Dalton's waterfront. On this side of the street, we supplied anything a man wanted – women, drink, gambling, opium was all yours if you could pay for it. If you could not, you ended up on the other side.' I looked at the other side where the dirty grey water lapped at the stone of the quay.

'Ye drowned them?' I asked, horrified.

'No. No profit in that. See that ship at anchor? That belongs to Dalton. They ended up on that until the debt was paid. Most of what we supplied came in on that. Dalton liked the sea. He used to say it brought the goods in and the bads out.' We walked down the street. 'I went into the water over there,' Wexford said. 'A party for Dalton at Mammies. The invitation said you have to come.' We came to a door with a sign saying 'Mammies home for wayward girls'. Wexford knocked. A well-dressed woman opened the door.

'Welcome home, Cyril,' she said. 'Mr Doyle told me you were back.'

'Thanks, Mammie. The best in the house for me and my friend.'

'Sure, Cyril,' she said, leading us to a room with a table set for two; a large jug of wine sat in the middle of it. Wexford poured some.

'Drink, Mammie,' he offered it to the woman. 'I had nothing to do with what happened to you.'she said

'Drink,' Cyril repeated. She drank and handed him back the mug.

'You were a fool to come back, Cyril.'

'Send them in one at a time,' Cyril said. He offered me some wine.

'Sit,' he said, 'and enjoy.' I sat and looked around. The walls were hung with rich red curtains with pictures of naked women in between. I was enjoying them when a curtain parted a real woman stood there. She was dressed head to toe in a red robe, tied at the waist. I gaped at her. I had never seen anything so beautiful. Her hair was piled up, making her seem six-foot tall. She pulled the knot on her robe; it slipped to the floor. She wore a chain around her waist and another on her neck. Boots that ended mid-thigh. Apart from that, she was naked. I stared at her as Wexford laughed. My mouth hung open. Her skin was as black as coal.

Wexford whispered something to Mammie. They were looking at me, amused. I tried to hide my surprise by saying, 'Bishop Watkins would not like her.' Wexford said, 'Next'. The woman smiled in our direction, picked up her robe and left, to be replaced by another, and another.

'Do you see anything you like?' he asked me.

'I haven't seen anything I did not,' I said in truth. The next was fully clothed, and I was about to protest at this oversight, when I recognised Marg.

'So,' she said. 'Your back to this?' she sounded defeated.

'Well, that's what you believed when I disappeared, was it not?' Wexford accused her.

'No,' she said. I thought you dead. I never believed what they told me until you walked through the door, alive. What else would keep a man from his wife for ten years, if he loved her?'

'Love, Marg, got me in the water across from here. I thought it was the end, but the only thing that was on my mind was not seeing you again to say goodbye. It took me ten years to get the strength to return. Then I find I have a son who calls Doyle 'daddy'. She flushed.

'I always knew Doyle wanted me, but while my father was alive I was safe. When he was killed, I had a son to take care of. I needed Doyle to run the business. I did what had to be done. He wanted to have you declared dead and marry me. I said I wanted proof you were dead. Tonight, I may well get that proof, Cyril. Please, leave.' I got to my feet.

'You have much to discuss. I will be in next room.' I breathed a sigh of relief as the door closed behind me. I was in a large room with the women I had seen earlier, draped on seats in various stages of undress. I saw Mammie behind the bar in the corner of the room and headed for her gratefully.

'Rum,' I said. 'Marriage?'

'Yeah,' she agreed.

'Quiet night,' I observed.

'It will be very busy later. Lots of soldiers in drinking dens on this street, building up courage.' 'For Cromwell, I asked?'

'No. For them.' She nodded in the direction of the girls.

'And you?' I asked. 'Are you not afraid of Cromwell?'

'They are men, and like all men they come, and they go,' she laughed.

'No,' I said, 'they are not like all men. Ye should leave this town for a while, until it's over.'

'Go with you, I suppose,' she said.

'Well, yes,' I said.

'My My,' she said. 'You are the greedy one. Violet,' she called. 'This one wants ye all. Take him and knock some of the ambition out of him.' Violet was the black lady. Despite my weak protest, she caught me by the arm and led me to a room which reminded me of O'Neill's jail. She dropped her robe, and again I was mesmerised by her strange exotic beauty.

'Strip,' she said. In a dream, I removed my clothes, my body reacting to her nearness and nakedness.

'You bold boy,' she said, picking up a riding crop and bringing it down smartly on my swollen manhood which promptly disappeared. I yelped and grabbed up my clothes as she landed one across my arse.

'Stop,' I yelled; she seemed mystified.

'But Cyril said you liked it.' Cyril Doyle would have to wait. I wanted him first. I was still pulling up my pants when I got to the main room, Violet still holding the whip as she apologised, and there they were. Doyle and his henchmen. Doyle said, 'Where is he?'

'You can't have him,' I said, 'he is mine.' Two of Doyle's gang headed for me. Mammie ran between us.

'You know the rules. All disputes to the street.' A door opened, and Wexford was there, pulling up his trousers as Marg looked over his shoulder.

'The street then, five minutes, or we are coming back in?' Doyle scowled in the direction of Marg. 'You made your bed,' he said. 'This town is mine now.' He stormed out with his henchmen.

'You,' I said, pointing my finger at Wexford.

'Yes?' he asked.

'You,' I said, pointing my finger in the direction of Violet. She was gone. 'You'. Marg was looking over Wexford's shoulder. 'You could maybe show us a back way out,' I finished tamely. 'You can't be afraid of Doyle and a few men,' said Wexford, heading for the door. As he passed me, he whispered, 'Violet, a bad habit. You will thank me someday.' I thought about hitting him. I thought about letting him go out alone. Still, in the end, I walked out beside him. There they were, Doyle and his men, standing with their back to the water.

'Is that them?' asked James, appearing at Wexford's elbow.

'That's them,' agreed Wexford. I looked right and left. A line of muskets and pistols were trained on Doyle and his men.

'What's happening?' I asked James.

'Back in our parish, I promised Wexford this day. He, in turn, promised a share in the spoils.' 'What spoils?' I asked.

'That we are about to find out,' said James. Wexford and James crossed the street, and I tagged along. 'Which one? asked James.

'That one,' said Wexford.

'Ah, Mr Doyle,' said James. 'I have under my command a good and trusted soldier who claims you have deprived him of the proceeds of his many businesses for ten years. He would like you to reimburse him.'

'Who is this little shit?' Doyle asked.

James continued, unfazed. 'He further claims the loss of three front teeth.' A huge fist flashed, catching Doyle square on the mouth; he would have gone in the water, but I grabbed him. James pried his mouth open.

'Three,' he pronounced. 'Very good, all do there could be some room for error in those matters. Where was I? Ah yes. A broken nose.' Wexford's fist flashed again. 'No error there,' said James. 'As luck would have it, you have only one nose. What was next?' James asked Wexford. 'The ribs or the stabbing?'

'The ribs,' Wexford said, 'but I was lying down for that.'

'We could break his legs,' said James, 'or we could ask him to lie down.'

'Ye are mad,' said Doyle.

'He speaks,' said Wexford, 'but not what I want to hear.'

'The legs then,' said James.

'Wait,' said Doyle. 'We can make a deal. I will give you all the coins I have if you leave me in peace; after all, it was Dalton who wanted you dead.' James and Wexford exchanged glances. 'We journey on tomorrow,' said James.

'Agreed,' said Wexford. They left to collect, taking Doyle and his men with them. I left them go. I thought of re-entry to Mammies, but the moment had passed. Rum. I remembered the warm feeling it produced. I walked down the street until I heard the sound of laughter and chatter coming from an establishment. I pushed in the door and walked in. I was halfway to the bar before I noticed the silence; looking around, I saw why — people who dressed grandly like me in Doyle's clothes did not come in here. I shrugged my shoulders. I was here now.

'Rum,' I said. An evil-looking man with a badly scarred face slapped a jug in front of me and sloshed some liquid into it. I pulled a coin out of my pocket and gave it to him. He looked at it and wordlessly took back the small mug he had given me and gave me the large one he had been pouring from. I looked into its murky depths, took a mighty slug, and waited for the warmth to spread from my toes, but it went the other way. It burned my mouth. It burned my throat. It burned my stomach. It burned all the way down to my toes, then it started back up – stomach, throat, mouth, and out; it hit a man's back who was leaning against the bar. The man shook himself. He had been dozing.. Slowly his hand moved to his back. He brought it around to his nose. His head jerked away from it. He nosed it again to make sure, then he turned slowly around, almost nose to nose with me. I felt something prick my stomach then was gone.

'Ah my friend,' he said, giving me a hug and kissing me on both cheeks. It was Greasy Garcia. On closer inspection of the customer's I recognised his men.

'Come,' he said. 'We will drink.'

'Not here,' I said. 'I know where the rum is rum.'

'Come,' he beckoned his men. 'We drink with my friend.' I could feel something trickle down my stomach, and put my hand inside my shirt. It came out red with blood.

'Sorry,' said Garcia. 'I did before I know you, my friend.' He flicked his wrist and a thin bladed knife appeared and disappeared from his sleeve.

'Someday, I show you,' he said.

'Yes, yes,' I said.

We had come to Dalton's. The rum was as I said. Greasy told me stories of piracy and murder, a father, captain of a trading ship, looted and sank by an English warship. He had been a cabin boy, a sailor and finally a captain who raided and plundered off the English coast, until a storm wrecked him off the Donegal coast.

'Here,' he said, 'I like I can smell the sea. I have rum; if only I have ship. Ship. Something stirred in my rum-laden brain.

'Ship,' I repeated. 'We will get a ship.'

'Where?' he said, looking around.

'You're drunk,' I accused him.

'Not,' he said.

'C,mon then. I will ship you a show.'

'You're drunk,' he accused.

'Not,' I said.

'I will show you a ship.' We left bumping, into each other for support. The rest followed. A few wrong turns, we arrived back at the waterfront.

'It's there,' I said, pointing out to sea. They all gathered round me, peering into the darkness. One of them voiced what was obvious.

'I can't see anything.'

'It's there,' I insisted. 'I saw it earlier, and my friend Wexford owns it, he won't mind if we look it,' I added. A feeling of goodwill had spread through me with the rum.

'You sure?' Greasy was looking up into my face. 'He would not think we might steal it, me being a pirate and all?' He belched and a little rum ran from the corner of his mouth.

'Course not,' I said grandly. 'It's out there and we are in here.'

'Boats,' said Greasy. They wandered up and down the quay.

'Here they are,' shouted one. We began to pile into the boats.

'Wait,' I said. 'How are we going to find it if we can't see it?' My mind coming to terms with the danger involved in twelve drunks rowing out to sea in the dark to a ship we can't see.

'I, Captain Garcia, can smell a ship a hundred yards away.' He took a deep breath, then said, 'I smell rum. Does this ship carry rum?' This did nothing to restore my confidence as we rowed out into the darkness.

'This reminds me of the night we raided the ship in the English harbour,' Garcia said to no one in particular. The one they called Skinny chimed in.

'Was that the night the dawn broke early and the harbour guns blew?'

'Shush,' said Greasy. 'I hear something.' We listened. I only heard the lapping of the water.

'Yes,' he whispered. 'We are near.'

'Why are we whispering?' I whispered.

'Did you tell your friend we were coming on board?' he whispered.

'No,' I whispered.

'Well then, it's best to sneak aboard in case the watch mistakes us for pirates,' he whispered. 'This reminds me of the night I was on watch. You were bringing back the two women,' Skinny said, 'and I wasn't expecting you back. Remember? I shot one of them.

'One was enough. Now shut up. There it is.' Greasy, despite all his rum, had grabbed a rope and silently slithered up it, followed by the rest. I tied the rope to the boat and, standing up, caught it, but my weight shoved out the boat and I landed in the water up to the waist, clinging grimly onto the rope. I inched my way up the side of the ship, then they started to pass me, legs and arms flailing as they splashed into the sea below. As my eyes drew level with the deck, I saw Greasy heading for the rope I was hanging from with a knife. I heaved myself onto the deck just as he cut it and threw it over the side. Then he saw me.

'Ahh, my friend. I could not convince them your friend owns the ship, so I give them a small boat to check.' We looked, and sure enough, they were rowing away hurriedly.

'In the morning, we sail,' he said, his whole face was beaming with happiness. We organised a watch in case there was an attempt to retake. I volunteered, as sleep was out of the question. I found a lantern on deck, lit it up and began to wander around. I admired the huge wheel that was lashed in place; as we were at anchor, I opened a chest in front of it containing a flag. I held the light close. I had seen it somewhere before. Next to the chest was a hatch. It was bolted. I undid the bolt and descended the stairs into pitch darkness. I felt something flat and left the lantern down on it until my eyes adjusted to the dimness. Something was written on what I now could see was a barrel. I slowly spelled it out: g, u, n, p, o, w, d, e, r. I caught the lantern and lifted it. I was surrounded by gunpowder, barrels and barrels of it. I eased my way back up the deck, closing the hatch behind me. Further along, another hatch; this time, muskets, pistols, cannon-shot. We were loaded with munitions, but for who? Not for Wexford, or they would be on shore. The answer came at dawn. As the fog lifted, three ships blocked the entrance to the harbour. They were flying the flag of the parliamentary army – the flag in the chest. I went below. The smell of stale rum and other offen-sive odours made my stomach churn, but I persisted. A bell hung near the stairs. I gave it a strong shake, and they were on their feet, staring at me with varying degrees of menace.

'Dawn,' I said. Greasy brightened.

'We sail,' he declared.

No,' I said. His eyes narrowed.

'We sail,' he repeated as he brushed past me. 'I owe you much,' he said. 'Your brother he save our life you get me ship.' He ran up the stairs. I followed. 'How could I leave ye?' he finished, his eyes fixed on the warships blocking the harbour.

THE SIEGE OF WEXFORD

'The land army can't be far behind,' I said. 'We need to know our men have left.'

'Why?' asked Garcia. 'Why can't we fight here?'

'We fight no one,' I said. 'Here we run.'

'Run, run,' Garcia said. 'I am tired of running.'

'See those ships?' I said. 'They have cannon. Look up the quay. What do you see? Cannon. Look in the hold.' He walked over, opened, looked in.

'We fight no one,' he agreed.

'Doyle knows we have the ship. He will never let us leave with a cargo worth a fortune. Break out the muskets. We will have to wait it out. James will know what to do.' I took the remaining boat and made my way to shore. Daytime. The waterfront looked and smelled bad. Large groups of armed men patrolled the streets. Cannons were being moved into position. I fell into step with a group of soldiers who seemed to be going in the right direction – Dalton's. I went around the back to the stables. Sleepy looked at me with a jaundiced eye as I fed him. Wexford's horse was still there. I went in the back door to Dalton's, up the stairs, knocked on number ten. Wexford poked his head out, blinked and said, 'Why are you still here?'

'Where is James?' I asked.

'New Ross,' Wexford said. 'We are to meet there.'

'What about Doyle?' I asked.

'He gave what he had, said no hard feelings and left. I paid some soldiers to guard the place last night.'

'I walked straight in,' I pointed out.

'Never any trouble daytime. The clergy would shut down the brothels and bars, and there would be nothing left to fight over,' Wexford pointed out.

'Things have moved on,' I said. 'Out in that harbour, Garcia is in your ship surrounded by warships sitting on an explosive fortune. Wexford blurted, 'That's why Doyle was so easy to deal with. His money is invested in the war. We have to get out before Cromwell's army closes in. Marg, time to go,' called Wexford. Marg and her son left in a horse and trap, with Wexford riding behind. They were not the only ones, as mostly well-dressed women and children passed through the gates, leaving behind the poor who had nowhere else to go. I tied Sleepy to the trap and said, 'I must go back to Garcia.' I walked around the walls, admiring the strong wall and stout gates, and concluded Cromwell would suffer should he throw his men against those defences; but at the back of my mind was the stout walls of Drogheda. The day after, Cromwell called on Wexford to surrender; they refused, and the cannons roared. A breach was made in the wall. A troop of Cromwell's soldiers dressed in black chanting some prayer flung themselves at it. They suffered heavy losses, but showed that the town was not as safe as it seemed. The town entered into negotiations with Cromwell for terms. This I was told by a troop that I had joined on the walls. Next day, they attacked again. This time, some got through but were put to the sword by a troop who reinforced any place along the wall that was breached. At the end of the day we were relieved. Word spread that terms were agreed and tomorrow we would be at peace. On our way back for much-needed sleep, we passed Doyle and his men heading for the wall. We woke to the sound of screams. We grabbed our arms and ran into the street. Cromwell's soldiers were in the town hacking their way down the street. Those who managed to get out of their houses, old men, women and children, ran in front of them. The soldiers flowed down the street like a river of death in and out of homes, leaving nothing alive in their wake. Our captain tried to organise a line of resistance, but the terrorised citizens broke our lines, and we fled with them.

'The waterfront,' I shouted to the captain. 'We can defend the alleys.' He shouted orders and we turned off the street into the alleys. We engaged them then, but they seemed more interested in the slaughter than engaging us.

'Boats, boats,' I shouted. 'Anything that floats, that ship is friendly.' We backed towards the waterfront, a wedge of steel. The captain had dispatched men, and boats began to arrive. Tables were also thrown into the water. I ran to the quay waving my arms. Garcia was already raising sail, coming in as close as possible. We piled into the boats; those that could swim jumped in, others grabbed tables and paddled desperately towards the ship. The main body of Cromwell's troops were pouring through the alleys. Some had started to load muskets and were intent on picking us off as we floundered in the water. The ship was in range now, and Garcia's men opened up with lines of muskets, and the would-be marksmen were put to flight, leaving several of their numbers behind. They were in the brothel. You could hear the screams. Mammie ran out the door, pursued by two men. She got to the quayside.

'Jump,' I shouted. 'Jump'. Too late. A slash of a sword and her head hung sideways as she fell in the water. Violet was next, but not the Violet I knew. She was holding a baby. One of them grabbed her, one took the baby and slapped it off the wall, then took his sword and ran it through her again and again.

'I told you. I told you. These men are different.' I was crying as we climbed aboard the ship. They were running along the quay, stopping only to dispatch the poor wretch's who were slow to choose the sea rather than the sword. The ones running along the quay were shouting at their comrades on the wall and pointing at our ship. A cannon was loaded, and its barrel lowered to our ship's line of approach. I could see the flare of the torch. A hand caught the torch and flung it over the wall. Doyle, who was now wearing the trappings of a Cromwellian officer, gave us a mock salute as we passed.

'Why?' asked the captain who was stood beside me.

'The ship,' I said, 'and the value of the cargo. He expects to get it back. We are going inland.'

THE NECKLACE

We were going nowhere. Garcia had one of his men dropping lead for depth; after which, he dropped anchor and announced grimly, 'We will have to go back with the tide, or we will be grounded. Like it or not, we have to run the blockade. Get through those ships to open sea.' Henry the captain of the soldiers shook his head.

'Not possible. If we avoid their cannon, there are the sandbanks. Only the harbour master could guide you through them. In daylight, at that,' he added.

'Captain Garcia will find a way through the sandbank,' Greasy said, 'but the ships,' he shrugged. 'We would have to go between them; even in darkness, their lights will pick us up in time to man their cannon. One hit in our hold the gunpowder would blow us to hell.'

'Bad stuff that gunpowder,' said a voice behind me. 'Do you remember the time we sold the English sailor the tobacco with the little shake of gunpowder in it. Blew his beard clean off. Nothing left of it but sparks.' It was him again; a long string of misery they called Skinny. Garcia said, 'That was because they gave us the free rum. They said they would give us another if we could drink it and turn the mug upside down in two seconds.'

'Did you?' I asked, my new-found interest in rum sparking the question.

'Yes,' said Garcia, and stopped.

'There was a note on the bottom of the mug,' said Skinny. 'Tell him what the note said captain,' asked Skinny.

'We pissed in it,' Garcia said, looking daggers at Skinny; but Skinny was not for stopping.

'Or the time you made the necklace for that English captain with the posh voice. Four pouches filled with gunpowder wrapped around his neck with the cord dangling down to his waist. You were asking him where he hid the valuables. You said, 'Talk'. He said, 'Never'. You lit the cord to frighten him, but it took off. We jumped behind the desk just in time; even so, we were covered in bits of brain. Garcia was not listening; he had become thoughtful.

'The necklace might work,' he said, heading for Skinny who paled and said, 'I will shut up.' Garcia grabbed him.

'Yes. The necklace might work, but this time we need to know the speed of the burn. Get in a boat.' With the tide starting to go out, we spent an hour letting Skinny float away with a rope of various lengths dipped in oil, until at a distance of three hundred yards the rope burned out. The plan was: two boats loaded with gunpowder tied eighty-foot apart, rowed into position, fuse lit and let drift

140

to catch on the ship in the centre of the channel and explode, letting us slip through to face the sandbank.

'What about the other ships?' Henry the Wexford captain said.

'We hope we will be through the sandbanks before they can bring their guns to bear,' Garcia answered.

'Do another necklace, for the one nearest quay,' Henry requested. 'I will row it into position where the ship is anchored. Then I will release the boats.' Garcia ordered the second necklace.

'I will row the one to bring you back,' I said.

And so it was. The night came in, and the tide went out. We went with it. We prepared the boats. Henry and I left first, as the boat near the harbour was the furthest away from our ship. We rowed past the walls and came in sight of the quay; the murderous horde were not yet sated. A gallows had been erected on the quay. A line of hapless prisoners awaited a brief trial, which seemed to have only one verdict. Then a body which had stopped twitching was removed from the gallows to make room for the next, who, in turn, had to witness the beheading of the previous victim while being strangled. Henry, who rowed beside me, said quietly, 'All my family are in there. I should join them.' I looked at him worriedly.

'You can't do anything for them,' I said. 'They are beyond help.' We rowed on past the fluttering robes of a priest who was the current occupier of the gallows. Killer and victim serving the same god – one was seeking sanctuary after his death, the other seeking favour for his murder; like all my kind, raised on superstition. I wished for proof that there was a forgiving god, but could only find signs of the existence of Satin. When I dragged my eyes away from the quay, Henry was gone – one of the gunpowder boats was gone with him. . He was going to row the boat into the ship and go up with it, to join his family, leaving me with a boatload of gunpowder on tow on the wrong side of the harbour. A feeling of panic came over me, water was new to me, water in the dark frightened me. I pondered my options. Rowing with the tide alone, would I get back to the ship before it set sail, and where was the necklace? I had only one chance. I rowed with all my strength with the tide, aiming between the lights of the two near ships. I passed between them unnoticed. I had just cleared them when the first necklace exploded, and the one in the middle, which I had just passed, seemed to lift out of the water. Timber and sparks flew into the air and began to fall all around me. With a yelp, I realised my danger. A smouldering plank had landed in the gunpowder boat. I grabbed the rope and hauled it in, grabbing the plank and throwing it into the sea. Henry set off his boat just then. His boat had been positioned well, not so many flashes, but the ship quickly sank. Garcia was on the move now. No sail, just drifting with the tide as they dropped lead for depth from the one remaining lifeboat. But the burning remains of the stricken ships had lit up the harbour, had exposed Garcia, and the ship on the far side of the harbour was weighing anchor and raising sail. I rowed madly to catch up. Skinny had found the channel, and up went the sails. I watched them sail away from me. I looked behind. The enemy ship was lining up for the channel. My first panicked thought was to get rid of the gunpowder and strike for shore. I cut the rope, then it came to me – I could make an anchor. I pulled in the gunpowder boat, got a barrel, tied the rope to it, and dropped it over the side. Then I looked at the fast-approaching ship. Five minutes, I thought. I cut the fuse, lit it, and rowed madly away. As I did, I looked backwards – the gunpowder-laden boat was following me. With a squeak of terror, I redoubled my efforts. When I fearfully looked again, the anchor had caught. I was putting distance between it and me; not so the following ship, as it bore down on it. They saw it, the burning fuse giving it away. I heard a shout. The ship tacked sharply as the gunpowder went up. A blast of hot air hit me, followed by a wave that threatened to swamp me, but did not. The ship was still there. One of the sails was on fire. It was quickly brought down. I rowed for the shore. Fearfully, I looked back; the ship had not moved. It was on the sandbank. Garcia was free to sail away.

THE VILLAGE

I beached the boat and ran. Would they come after me? I did not think so, but I ran just the same. The fear driving me on until I could run no more. Then I walked and stumbled through the darkness, looking for shelter. I was cold now, the night chill taking hold. A farm, a reek of hay; that was enough. I lay in at its butt and pulled enough hay out to cover me. I slept the sleep of exhaustion. Violet was bending over me. She was telling me how sorry she was. I told her how sad I was, how I did not understand. She was just a mother doing her best to provide for her baby. I could feel her soft, moist lips on my cheek; then she kissed me harder, her tongue sliding along my face into my hair and pulling it; the pain woke me up. I was looking into a pair of large brown eyes in a bony face with horns. A cow. This I discovered by looking underneath her. She had a fine doug of milk. After talking to her gently and scratching her tail, I knelt and caught a teat, aimed it in the direction of my mouth, and squeezed; it shot milk up my nose; a small correction and into my mouth. The coldness started to leave me as the warm milk hit my stomach.

'That's a fine calf you have there, Nora.' The woman's voice came from behind me. I looked around, startled; the jet of milk sizzling into my ear. A small, wiry woman was standing there, pitchfork in hand. I looked at it then back to the woman.

'I came for some hay,' she said. 'You are welcome to the milk. It's the only thing we have plenty of.'

'I will get it for you,' I said. She hesitated, then handed me the fork. I peeled a layer of hay from the cock.

'Where do you want it?' I asked. She led me to a stone wall where what I presumed was Nora's calf stood waiting patiently for his hay.

'Eggs and brown bread,' she said, looking me up and down.

'What?' I said.

'Eggs and brown bread,' she repeated.

'Yes,' I said, my mouth watering. I followed her. She opened the door to a hovel. Hens flew out. 'Henhouse?' I asked.

'Home,' she said. 'Fox,' she added.

'Aah,' I said. There were four eggs in a nest inside the door. The nest was the bottom drawer of the dresser. The upper part contained some mugs and plates, safe from where the hens roosted, which was the edge of the top drawer, which was pulled out so the hens could shit into it. I was impressed. I had never seen such a practical use of a dresser. A turf fire was burning in the open fireplace that took up half the room. The entire floor was stone, rubbed smooth by years of wear. She was looking at me again. 'Up there'. I looked up the chimney. A small side of bacon hung there. I unhooked it.

'Cut,' she said, handing me a knife. I knew this was all she had, so I cut two thin slices and put the bacon back on the hook. She threw the two pieces into a flat pan, turned them, then broke the eggs over them. She pulled a loaf of brown bread from the pot beside it and said, 'Cut'. I cut two huge lumps as it fell apart.

'Butter in the dish,' she said. A dish lay on the rough timber table. I opened it, and put large dollops on the hot brown bread. She plonked two plates on the table. 'Grace,' she said. I led her in the prayer. 'Priest?' she asked. I looked at her alarmed. 'The way you said grace,' she explained.

'Altar boy,' I said.

'Ahh,' she said. We ate in silence. Afterwards, I stood up awkwardly.

'Thanks for the food. I will be on my way.' She came to the door to watch me leave.

Further along, I passed other cottages like hers; small-holdings with walled-in corn patches. Children were playing, women hanging out washing, bringing in turf. I caught a head of corn. The seed fell out in my hand; it was none of my business. Their menfolk would harvest it. My pace slowed. I had not seen any men. I stopped and turned. I could see her in the distance, still standing at the door watching me. I walked back to her.

'Where are the men?'

'Gone,' she said. 'Gone with the priest. He told them it was their duty to defend their faith.' 'Where did they go?' I insisted, knowing the answer but not wanting to hear it. She was looking into my face.

'Wexford,' she said. 'They went to Wexford.'

'Did this priest say when they would be back?' I asked, trying to cover up what she may have seen in my face.

'No,' she said.

'Well the corn needs to be cut now. Scythes?' I asked. She gathered the women. We began the harvest. I did most of the cutting, the women tied it into sheets and brought it to the threshing floor, where women took turns with the flails knocking the grain free. It was gathered and bagged. It was both food and seed for next year. It was all I could do. I began to wonder how many around Drogheda, around Wexford, around Ireland would die, not by Cromwell's soldiers, but by the famine which would surely follow. I slept wrapped in a blanket in front of the fire in Mary's house, while she slept in the bed in the corner, hidden by a sheet hanging from the ceiling. The next day while cutting, the women looked at me strangely and would go into small groups whispering to each other. When darkness fell, some of them called Mary aside. Words were exchanged. She came to me and said, 'They do not think it right you sleeping in my house.'

'Ask them which of them has a room,' I said. She departed, and a whispered consultation began. Mary came back.

'No one has a place for you.'

'So I sleep with Nora again,' I said.

'I told them to go to hell,' said Mary. The next day they came to me and asked me to leave. My presence in Mary's house was spreading scandal, the talk of the parish, and when Tom, Mary's husband, came home, it would go hard on her. I told them I would leave when the corn was in, and that Mary was safe, and explained to them that the expert application of a whip was required before I could produce what was needed for mounting. They left with gasps and screams, amid prayers and threats to tell Fr O'Brien when he returned. We finished that day, as the work's speed increased greatly, even though the women took a wide route passing me while regarding me with horror. That night I told Mary I would leave in the morning. She was studying me.

'Is it true?' she asked.

'What?' I asked.

'That you have problems.'

'I have lots of problems,' I said. Red-faced, she persisted. 'Whip, mounting', her face getting redder.

'Yes I had a problem with whips and mounting,' I said, trying not to laugh.

'We don't have children,' she said. 'Tom and me. Tom has a problem. I could help you if you help me.' There it was, out in the open.

'What would Fr O'Brien say?' I asked. 'Or your neighbours?'

'I don't care,' she said. 'I want a baby.'

'No you don't,' I said. 'There's a war on.' I told her the story of Violet, a woman with a baby. A woman alone who would do anything for her baby. At the same time, unknowing men used her body any way they wished. She was above it; she was doing it for her baby. I told her of how it ended, years running down my face. She came and held me. She kissed my cheek softly and whispered into my ear.

'It was Wexford, wasn't it?'

'They are not coming back,' I said. 'They are all dead.'

Before I left the next day, she made a point of hugging me in full view of the village. She said, 'You are a good man. Don't let them change you.' I passed closed doors and turned backs. When I got to the end of the village, I looked back. Mary had come out of the house dressed from head to toe in black. She walked to the first house, and when the wailing started I walked away. After what seemed endless hours of walking and hiding, for I trusted no one, there it was below me, New Ross; and my spirit lifted, for there in the bay was Garcia's ship.

NEW ROSS

Ijoined the busy road, glad I was near shelter, as the weather had worsened and a small stream of rainwater kept pace with me as I walked into the town. The heavens opened again as I passed a church. I entered. A priest was saying Mass. I went through the motions and wanted it to matter. I prayed that I could return to what I once was, an innocent man of the land, a man who could live a life of peace, without kings or parliaments, without people who could follow the words of a man of peace and find in them a reason to kill. The priest mounted the pulpit to give his sermon.

'We are gathered here to pray, to pray for the people of Wexford, who gave their lives for the faith. We will pray for them, but do they need our prayers? For they have gone to their eternal reward, along with their martyred priests. It now falls on us to take up arms to defend New Ross, to defend the faith.' I had heard enough. I got to my feet to walk out. 'Yes,' the priest thundered. 'Let the cowards walk out, let them turn their back on their priest.' I looked around. I was the only one standing. 'Soon he will turn his back on his god. Then he will suffer the fires of eternal damnation.' I turned. All heads were watching me. I ignored the priest.

'I have come from a village where a priest such as this inspired the menfolk to go to Wexford town to defend the faith. Only women and children are left there. With my help, they will get through this winter. Who will get them through the next? Go home. Take care of your wife, your children. This war can't take your faith from you, but it can take your lives and that of your families.' The priest was not happy with me addressing his flock.

'If you do not care to listen to what I have to say, why have you come in here?' he challenged. To find peace, I thought, to find myself.

'It was raining,' I said. 'It was raining.' I walked on. I needed a place to stay, a place to rest. First, food – a sizable portion of bacon. Later, I asked the serving lady where I might find a room. She gave me directions, advising me to avoid a nearby street as it had been taken over by an unruly element. I smiled to myself. I had found my friends. I walked the short distance to the forbidden street. A cart had been drawn across the entrance, blocking all but where two armed thugs lounged. I went to brush past them, but one of them put a hand on my chest.

'Where you think you are going?' he asked.

'Up the street,' I said. He held out his hand. I shook it. They looked at each other.

'You ever here before?' one asked. I shook my head.

'Well,' he explained, 'you have to pay to get into this street.'

'Why?' I asked.

'To keep out undesirables,' he said. I looked them both up and down.

'Didn't work did it,' I said. They both looked puzzled.

'Wat ya meen?'

'Never mind,' I said. 'Would you tell the ugly one with the flat nose and missing teeth that I am here, as this sounds like his work. He is called Wexford,' I added.

'No one here by that name,' said one.

'Sounds like Cyril,' said the other.

'Tell Cyril I am here,' I said.

'Go on in. First alehouse.'

The first alehouse had 'Cyril's' in large letters over the door. The noise hit me as I entered. Three sweating barmen served the thronged room, with serving women doing the tables while dodging the drunken attentions of the customers. One fellow grabbed at a woman to stop his drunken descent to the floor, taking the front of her blouse with him. There was whoops of approval, but a truncheon landed on his head, and he went past me in the hands of a man dressed like a king. As the unfortunate man was flying through the door, Wexford turned to me and said, 'What kept you?' His smile was entire. Three gold teeth filled the gap. I leaned closer. Had someone tried to straighten his nose? He led me to the bar.

'Rum for my friend. We will talk. Later.' I drank the rum and wandered out. I had not gone far when I came to Mammies. The ladies in the doorway left me in no doubt what it was. I wondered was it a coincidence or a tribute. Next was a shop, 'Garcia's', with pistols and muskets. The next was baths, a half dozen baths with curtains surrounding. I approached the kiosk to pay. It was Skinny.

'I give you the good-looking one,' he said.

'I thought all the baths looked the same.' I undressed and got in the bath. The curtains parted behind me and I closed my eyes as the warm water was poured over me. Soft hands rubbed soap on my back, then began to move around to the front. My eyes popped open. It was a woman. I grabbed myself and stuttered, 'What you doing here?'

'Skinny said you were to get whatever you want; what do you want?' she leaned over and her gown fell open. I dragged my eyes away.

'More water. Tell Skinny I want more water.' Out on the street again. Landers' hotel. I walked in. A lady in a flowing gown approached me.

'You must be Mr Landers. James said you were to be looked after. Come with me.'

'Where are we going?' I asked suspiciously.

'To your room, sir,' she said. She opened a door to a room with a large bed with rugs on floor and curtains on the windows.

'Is there anything else you would like, sir?' she asked. I warily said, 'No'.

'Your brother wishes to see you in the gentleman's club. You may wish to change,' she indicated the wardrobe. I opened it and looked inside. A choice of grand clothes and boots. I returned to the lobby. The lady looked me over with approval.

'Gentleman's club. Third on left, sir,' she said. A door-
man ushered me in. A crowd of prosperous men sat at tables drinking and smoking. One of them was James.

'What's all this?' I asked.

'Our friend Cromwell has retired to Dublin for the winter, so we have decided to stay here For this purpose we acquired some property on this street. When we opened our
businesses most of the others sold to us. This is our street,
our laws apply here. Garcia speaks very highly of you. He
says you saved his ship.

'I thought he would sail away,' I admitted.

'Well, he might well have done, but where better to sell
arms than here?' The voice came from behind me.

'And there was the problem of the men you saved not
wanting to go to sea,' he added a touch wistfully. I turned.
It was Garcia, hair tied back and washed, dressed in style,
but strangely looking more of a thief than ever. Garcia
flung his arms around me, kissing me on both cheeks. I
stepped back, alarmed, bumping into Wexford who had
just joined us.

'I am glad too,' said Wexford, reaching out for me, lips
puckered.

'You can kiss my arse,' I said, helpfully turning it towards
him. James was irritated.

'Why are ye like this?'

'Because he is trouble and I am the one he unloads it on,'
I replied.

'How can you say that?' Wexford cried. 'You went back
to Wexford, nearly got yourself killed, then feared drowned
and I was not within miles.'

154

'Doyle was,' I pointed out.

'Doyle?' Wexford echoed. 'What about Doyle?'

'He let them in,' I said.

'We should have killed him,' said James.

'He wanted it all,' said Wexford with a strangely calm voice. 'Well, he got nothing. We took his ship. He unleashed a crowd of madmen chanting passages from the Bible. It took three days for them to convert his town and everyone in it to ash. All Doyle got was an officer's uniform and a drab one at that.'

'That does not sound like Doyle,' Wexford mused.

'There must be something else. Marg might know,' I said, thinking out loud. Wexford's fist caught me on the jaw, and stars flashed before my eyes. I was up, a great relief flowing through me. The frustration of what seemed a lifetime followed my fist to his mouth. With great satisfaction, I felt the gold teeth dislodge before he hit me again. I went backwards over a table, legs in the air. He was coming around the table when they grabbed him.

'What was that about?' asked James.

'Ask him,' I said. 'I was only saying his wife knows Doyle.' He was coming at me again, but they held him.

'She might know something,' I finished tamely, knowing I could have put it better.

'Shake hands and apologise,' James ordered.

'I like Marg,' I said. 'I would not do anything to hurt her.' I held out my hand. He looked at it suspiciously, then shook it. I picked the gold teeth off the floor and handed them to him.

'Sorry,' I said, but the ghost of a smile escaped me, and he was getting angry again. James said, 'Well, ask Marg.'

'Ask Marg what?' Marg had come in off the street and was standing there, hands on hip. 'Ask me what, Cyril?'

'Marg,' he started.

'Where are your teeth?' she interrupted.

'In my pocket,' he answered sheepishly. She cast her eye around the room. It fixed on my blackening eye. She walked over to me, her nose almost touching mine.

'Ask me what?' I looked around the room for help; none was forthcoming.

'I just thought you might know something about Doyle.' Stars again as I received an open-handed swipe which hurt my already bruised jaw and crashed into my nose, sending tears down my cheeks. She turned towards Wexford.

'You promised you would not mention Doyle again.'

'But,' Wexford started, pointing towards me.

'Well, what do you want to know about Joseph?' Her temper was rising. But it suited her. 'To me he was gentle and caring. No one slighted me and got away with it. He was a good lover and wanted to marry me.'

'Ha,' said Wexford in derision.

'Yes, he did. He had several meetings with the bishop to have you declared dead. What more do you want to know?' she asked Wexford, who I now felt sorry for. 'He was nice, but he was not you,' she finished. She was looking up into his face, but he was too stupid to hold her. She let a cry and ran out.

'Go after her,' I pleaded, but his thoughts were elsewhere.

'The bishop,' Wexford exclaimed. 'What would Doyle be doing with the bishop?

'Put it another way,' James said. 'What had Doyle that the bishop might want?'

'The ship,' I said. 'It has to be the ship. But not the contents, or they would have been unloaded. The ship was to be used to take something out for the bishop. The bishop would not trust Doyle; the cargo would be heavily guarded.' James was getting interested. 'Solution. Open the gates. No guards, no bishop. Is it possible Doyle is sitting on something so valuable he gave up his town for it? And with Cromwell's troops now in the town and no ship, he can't move it.'

'Well, if there is a fortune in Wexford,' I pointed out, 'we have no idea where it is.'

'Doyle knows,' James said.

'He is not going to tell us anything,' I pointed out.

'I think maybe he will talk to us,' James concluded, 'when we bring back his ship.'

PAPAL GOLD

We sailed into Wexford harbour and anchored outside cannon range. Garcia hoisted the parliament flag. We could see people watching from the quay. Days past with no approach.

'What now?' I asked James, who was leaning on the rail looking towards the quay.

'We may be wrong, or we are playing a game of patience. Normally the first to move loses, but maybe not this time. Garcia, make ready to sail.' Garcia began to shout orders. 'Slowly,' added James. The anchor was slowly lifted. Sailors went aloft to inspect the sails. A figure on the quay left at the run. He came back with others. One of them was Doyle. Five men got into a boat, four rowed. Doyle sat in the front looking towards us. We threw him a rope ladder and he climbed aboard. He was the first to speak.

'God, I am glad to see you and my ship.'

'My ship,' Wexford corrected.

'Your ship, my ship. What matter? It is good to get away from that shower of lunatics.'

'Bad for business are they?' mocked Wexford.

'You would not believe it,' Doyle said. 'Everything is a sin. They go around quoting from the Bible, looking for people to kill. They still find the odd misfortunate. Did you ever read the Bible?' Cyril Wexford shook his head. 'Everyone in there has. They claim our priests got it wrong, making them and the Irish who believe the priests so far gone that every one of us they kill is a blessing. They are coming around to the belief that I may not be as holy as I should be. They need food. With the ship, we could trade with them. I will need to rebuild the business when they are gone.' 'We have what we came for,' James said. 'You. Ormond has offered a substantial reward for the traitor who opened the gates of Wexford. He wants to make an example of you.'

'Hung, drawn, quartered I heard mentioned,' I added. Doyle was looking from one to the other. 'What are ye talking about?'

'We are claiming the reward on your head, put up by the friends of Wexford, for the traitor who opened the gates.'

'What's that got to do with me?' Doyle asked.

'You opened them,' said James.

'Who said so?' asked Doyle.

'I did,' I said.

'Did you see me open the gates?'

'No,' I admitted, 'but I saw you and your men going to guard the gate; then in the morning, you were with them.'

159

'Yes, I was with them. I was working for them, shipping arms. I had slipped out to arrange delivery and collect a payment. I also brought them the news the town was about to surrender. Why would I open the gates? I had everything under control, then they got in and destroyed my business s.' 'That does not matter,' said James. 'You are a traitor. We will collect on you.'

'Maybe he did not open the gates,' I said. 'We could do him a favour.'

'What favour?' asked Wexford in a hostile voice.

'Well, we could kill him here,' I said. 'Nobody said he had to be alive. I would not like to hand anyone over to that mob that lost family in Wexford. Besides, he might jump overboard or escape and we would end up with nothing.'

'You are not as stupid as you look,' said Wexford in admiration. 'I will do it.' He drew a knife. 'Nice to my wife, were you?' He advanced in Doyle's direction. 'Nice and gentle, were you?' We could see he was building up to savagery.

'Wait, wait,' said Doyle.

'Don't worry. I will kill you slow,' said Wexford, giving him that smile that did not reach the eyes. 'I can make us all rich.' It came out in a gush.

'You would say anything to save yourself, wouldn't you?' said Wexford, still moving towards him. 'It is true,' Doyle was panicking.

'Wait,' it was James. 'Let him talk.'

'I have gold and coins. Lots of it.' He looked around at us, looking for a response.

'Your men are waiting in the boat,' said James. 'Send them for it. You can buy your freedom.' Expression after expression chased across Doyle's face.

'They can't get it,' he whispered fearfully.

'Ha,' said Wexford, producing the knife again.

'It is there,' his voiced rising as Wexford reached for him.

'Where?' asked James.

'In the church, it is in the church. Enough to pay an army, a Papal army.'

'Why has it not been looted?'

'They don't know it is there.' Doyle was starting to recover.

'But you do,' prompted James.

'Yes, I do,' said Doyle.

'Then why have you not taken it?' James again.

'It's under guard,' Doyle admitted.

'If they don't know it's there, why is it guarded?' James questioned.

'They stable the horses in the church. They guard the horses well, and the gold in the crypt. There is enough to make us all rich, but three hundred muskets are guarding it.'

'Then we have to get it out from under them, and onto this ship,' James mused.

'What if it's not there in the crypt?' I asked.

'Then Mr Doyle will lay in exalted company,' said James grimly. He began to pace up and down the deck, lost in thought. He stopped pacing and asked Doyle, 'To get it out and onto the ship, how long do we need?'

'A half-day maybe,' Doyle answered.

'That much?' asked James.

'That much,' said Doyle. James began to pace again, but nothing seemed to be happening.

'We could come back later with more men,' I suggested, 'maybe after Christmas.'

'Christmas,' James repeated. 'Christmas day. Yes,' he said. 'Christmas day. We have a week to set it up.' We took a while to talk it through when Doyle left Wexford and I went with him. The ship sailed back to New Ross to organise a Christmas party, while we rowed into the hell Wexford had become. They were waiting for us at the quay, some twenty of them led by a wild-eyed hulk of a man with a book in one hand and a sword in the other, a multi-coloured beard sprouted from his chin.

'Who are those heathen, devil worshippers?' was his first question to Doyle. He assured him that we were in fact hostages to be returned to the ship when the ship came back with much-needed supplies and oats for the horses, which he Doyle had paid for. We were to guarantee the ships return, and he, Doyle, would guard them till then. The wild eyes travelled from Doyle to us.

'Papists and idolaters,' he thundered.

'Scum,' added Doyle with some venom. 'We shall put them in their church with the horses, for God has decreed that they are no better than animals,' Doyle added.

'They shall see what has become of their place of evil worship,' the bearded one thundered. We were brought to the church and pushed in. As our eyes adjusted to the gloom we could see and smell the horses stabled there at night, but the smell of rotting flesh prevailed over all. Two figures hung from the ceiling. The smoke-blackened mitre jammed on the head of one proclaimed him a bishop. The bottom parts of the bodies had been burned to the bone by the pews, which had been set on fire. As we drew near, we could see bones amid the ashes. The walls were black from smoke and human grease.

'With god's help we will burn all ye heathen Irish in this life, and in hell the next,' the bearded one roared. I had seen it before they came to the church for sanctuary and to pray. The women and children. Only their bones remained. I looked sideways at Wexford, and what I saw was a man about to explode with mindless violence. I threw my arms around him. He struggled violently, but quickly realised that they were expecting and indeed hoping for a violent reaction so they could add our bones to the others.

'God has seen fit to give us a great victory over our enemies,' said the bearded one. Doyle joined in.

'If you doubt the rightness of our actions, I leave you this Bible. Read what God has decreed for places of evil such as this.' They left us with the dead in the carnal house of a lesser God.

'Well, we got into the church,' I said, hoping to cheer Wexford up, but his eyes were dull and distant.

'I will kill him,' he said. He was talking to himself. 'The one with the beard. I will kill him.' He shook himself and looked at me. 'Yes,' he said. 'We were lucky there. Now we start to clean up this mess.' We went to the door. The guards would not let us out, but got us shovels, and we began to shovel a mixture of bones, horse dung and ashes out the window. We cut down the corpses and, with the

163

help of shovels and a few boards, got them out the window. The place still smelt of death, but it was bearable. At dusk, they brought in the horses that had been grazing outside the walls and tied them on ropes around the church. We found a corner and slept as best we could. In the morning after the horses had been lead out, we cleaned out again.

'Now,' said Wexford. 'Where is this crypt?'

'You are from here,' I said. 'You should know.'

'Twelve years since I left, and before that I was not welcome. I was here as a child for Confirmation.'

'What did they name you for Confirmation?' I asked. He looked at me searchingly, saw no guile. 'Aloysius,' he said. I kept a straight face.

'Cyril Aloysius,' I exclaimed. 'They must have expected a lot from you.'

'Yes,' he said sadly, 'but both my parents worked for Dalton. Then they disowned me when I went to work for him. I bet they never thought I would be back here in this church.'

'Did you go to see them?' I asked.

'Never got around to it,' he admitted. 'Marg told them I was back; I got no invite,' he paused. 'They had left Dalton and taken to religion. I think they were happier praying for me when they thought me dead.' He was lost in the past. Then he shook himself. 'It's possible we shovelled them out the window.'

We were pacing the church, looking at the floor. A lot of notables had been buried underneath with their names engraved on the floor, but no sign of a possible entrance to a crypt. We were sitting eating some bread the guards gave us when Wexford began to tell of his days in the church, the problems getting married when he became Dalton's right-hand man.

'Marg did the leg work, she could charm anyone. I still cannot believe she chose me.'

'Me neither,' I said, but he let that pass.

'We stood up there at the altar and promised each other everything, and meant it. It was the happiest day of my life. Then we knelt on the step in front of the altar holding hands as the priest gave us the final blessing. I don't think I knelt since. Marg wanted me to go back, but the business,' he shrugged. 'It did not seem right. That did not stop our customers. They were up to confession, Communion and kissing the cross. Marg used to say if Jesus's feet were not nailed to the cross, he would kick them in the mouth. I looked to the altar trying to get a picture of Wexford and Marg on their wedding day.

'The floor,' I said. 'You knelt on the floor in front of the altar. There is no step in front of the altar.' He looked. 'There is a step at each side,' I pointed out, 'not in front.' We stood up and approached the altar.

'They moved it,' he said. 'The altar; they moved it.'

'Maybe to get closer to the people,' I said, but we were both thinking the same thing. I caught the corner of the marble and tried to slide it, but it did not move. Wexford quickly joined me, and it moved inches with a squeak which echoed around the church, and caused me to grab a shovel as a curious guard looked in the door. I ignored him and continued to scrape horse shit off the floor. 'You will be able to eat your dinner off that soon,' said the guard, his curiosity satisfied.

'It tastes like shit anyway,' I retorted, but we couldn't move the altar again. The guard appeared with a pot containing our dinner, a smile of selfcontentment on his face as he turned the pot upside down on the floor.

'Now you can eat your dinner off it.' You could hear them laughing outside as he recounted his joke to his fellow guards. We surveyed our dinner on a floor between scrapings of horse shit and grease from the burnt bodies. It was a stew; a few potatoes and large chunks of fat, the lean bits removed for better than us. Wexford leaned forwards and picked up the largest lump of fat, wiped some horse dung from it and stared at it.

'Are you going to eat that?' I said, my stomach knotting in revulsion. Wordlessly, he rose and walked to the altar. I followed. He knelt and began rubbing the fat on the floor. I was with him now, grabbing another piece and rubbing it on the floor around the altar. Then we stood and pushed, and the altar slid noiselessly back – and underneath was a large slab of stone with an iron ring in the middle. Wordless, we slid the altar back into position. The guards brought the horses back. They were still chuckling about the food on the floor. One asked had I cleaned the plate; stung I said, 'It will only give me a greater appetite for the Christmas day feast of geese, turkey and pork, followed by a copious amount of rum and whiskey. Then we will dance the dance of love, warmed by the great fire. Remember that when you see the flames not far from here, where ye will be as miserable as always.' Wexford nudged me to shut up. The guard's eyes narrowed.

'What is he talking about?' he inquired.

'Nothing. He goes like that,' Wexford said, giving me a dirty look. The guard left, but you could see he was not happy. The good feeling he had got from throwing our food on the floor was gone. We sat in the darkness, for hours not talking.

'I have to know,' said Wexford suddenly.

'Yes,' I said. 'Me too.' We slid the altar back. I felt my way to the nearest horse and undid the rope that held him. I brought him back to the iron ring, took off my belt, put around the horse's neck, tied the rope to the belt and then to the ring, and slowly walked the horse forwards by the mane. Wexford had robbed the hay from some horses and used it to silence the slab of stone as it flipped over. We looked down into the darkness.

'A candle would be nice,' I ventured. He was kneeling, feeling around with his hand.

'No steps,' he said. 'The rope. I got it.' He tied one end around his waist and disappeared down the dark hole.

'What's down there?' I asked when the rope went slack.

'Coffins,' he said. 'Lots of them.' My heart sank.

'That's what is usually in crypts,' I said sadly.

'Lots of coffins,' he repeated, 'very, very heavy coffins.' My ears picked up the excitement in his voice as he said, 'Pull me up.' I did. We walked to where a shaft of moon-light shone through the broken window. One coffin was open; he held up a chain. I caught it; its weight and where it was found telling me what it was. We whispered to each other. 'Gold'.

Doyle came to see us in the morning; with him came the bearded one and one of the guards.

'How was your lodgings asked Doyle.

'Basic,' Wexford retorted, 'with lousy food and service,' answered Wexford, eying up the offending guard, who smirked.

'Basic maybe,' went Doyle, 'but surely the peace and quiet of the church gave ye time to reflect on the wickedness of the life ye lead.'

'Amen,' went the bearded one, looking at Doyle with the pride a teacher reserves for his best pupil. 'Yea, brother,' I responded. 'The time spent here meditating hath opened our eyes to riches that cannot be described. When the ship returns, we will take with us our new-found faith, and share it with many.' Both Doyle's and the eyes of the bearded one lit up with pleasure. 'And ye shall slay all within these places, women, children and their animals, and you shall not take their riches, for they are evil.'

'Yes,' said the bearded one, 'so it is written,' his eyes shining.

'Your people are doing the Lord's work,' I continued. 'Now I know why we were never given a Bible to read while our heads were filled with lies.'

'We shall read together this evening,' said the bearded one, bestowing a great honour on me.

'I shall look forward to more revelations,' I said as he left. Wexford was looking up into my face. 'What was that?' he asked.

'That,' I said 'was a revelation. They send them in first to kill and get killed. Do the Lord's work or go to heaven, no retreat, no mercy. Somewhere behind them are people who know how to use them, and use them well.'

'When this war is over, who will claim them,' asked Wexford 'or us?' he added on reflection. They came for me as promised; a great gathering where the pages of the Bible were read. Praise God, and God is great,' they chanted in an eerie tone that seemed to send them into a trance. Then the bearded one stood up, held his arms up and cried.

'We have amongst us today a sinner who has read the good book and has seen the light. I call upon him to stand before us and lay bare his soul so it can be cleansed.' He came and led me into the centre of the crowd; I raised my hands.

'I have sinned.'

'Yea, brother,' they chanted.

'I have killed.'

'Yea, brother.'

'I have robbed.'

'Yea, brother.'

'I have frequented places of fornication, in the past.'

'Yea, brother.'

'I intended to attend the great druid feast at Poulnamucha on Christmas day; I stand ashamed before you,' I finished. The bearded one embraced me.

'Do you feel better now, my brother?'

'Yes,' I said. 'Yes', with as much fervour as I could muster.

'This feast on Christmas day,' he asked.

'I do not wish to speak of such evil,' I said, 'nor should you wish to hear it, for it would defile your ears.' I went to leave. He barred my way.

'Tell me,' he said.

'I cannot,' I said. 'I have put that sinful life behind me. But he knows of it, surely he has told you of this druid festival.' I pointed to Doyle. All attention shifted to Doyle.

'It's just and old custom,' said Doyle and stopped.

'Go on,' said the bearded one.

'They build a huge fire, and all the priests from the locality come and say high mass. Then, they preach to the gathering, telling them they should go home and leave the druid festival in the past.' 'What then?' asked the bearded one.

'The priests go home.' Doyle finished and turned to walk away.

'Tell them the rest,' I shouted, all eyes swung towards me and back to Doyle.

'The people honour the old gods of the druids. They dance naked around the fire. Then perform the rites of fertility.' Joshua recoiled in horror.

'Why have you not told us of this obscenity?' his beard bristling as he went nose to nose to Doyle. 'Because we are under orders to remain inside these walls until spring. I will follow those orders,' Doyle shouted.

'I, Joshua, follow a higher-order, and I will not be found wanting. I will purge this evil. If they dare to perform this pagan ritual, we will put them to the sword.' He pulled his sword and held it aloft, and all did the same with a great cry: 'God is good.'

We were all looking forward to Christmas; some to kill, some to rob, some to pray for forgiveness for mounting sins. The ship floated into the harbour on Christmas Eve morning, and the food for the garrison was brought ashore. Wexford and I were released from our prison and ate well as we waited for the boat to take us back to the ship. It was plain that we were not trusted; a large guard was placed on us until we left. Back on the ship, James was pacing the deck. He had hoped we would have been left ashore to prepare for our plan to remove the loot from the church. A guard of a dozen men armed with muskets watched us from the dock, men who had been in the company of Doyle. We believed we would be allowed to land when the time came to do so. Christmas morning, and the massive fire that James' men had set lit up the horizon, and we gathered on deck to see if our plan was working. A great commotion was taking place. Horses were being saddled, a gate opened and hundreds of soldiers poured out of Wexford led by the bearded Joshua.

'Man the boats,' said James. We piled into the boats and rowed towards shore. The guards opened fire on us. We were out of range; it was a warning. Doyle had joined them. From the town came the sound of battle, a cart drawn by two horses galloped through the gate. When it reappeared, the horses were straining at their harness under the weight of the coffins on the cart. Doyle shouted.

'I did open the gate this time. You see, the bishop's gold was for the nuncio's army. He asked a loyalist captain to guard it. The bishop did not trust me. The loyalists did not want a strong Irish Catholic army facing them when they regain power. We decided it was in both our interest to take it for ourselves. Thank you for your plan; it worked well. We will be leaving now; when Joshua returns, he will not be happy.' The guards and Doyle followed the cart joined by the loyalists fighting a rearguard action against the parliament troops as they left the town. We rowed back to the ship and hauled ourselves on board, disheartened.

'We were nearly rich,' said Wexford sadly. James was pacing the deck. He stopped and looked up river.

'We may still be rich. Garcia,' he shouted. Garcia came running. James was excited. 'Joshua will return within the hour. He will pursue them with the cart. Doyle can't outrun them.'

'What good is that to us?' I asked.

'Doyle is going to take the ferry,' James said. Garcia was the first to react, shouting and kicking his men into action. James was right. The first of the loyalists had reached the ferry and were bringing it back from the other side. We were sailing now towards the distant ferry which was being loaded with the cart. The ferry began to move. Two figures were with the cart – Doyle and the loyalist captain. Skinny was dropping lead.

'We will run aground,' he called to Garcia, who was at the helm. Garcia grabbed the nearest sailor, handed him the wheel, called two others who joined him in unwrapping a canvas, underneath which was the smallest cannon I ever saw. Powder was brought up on the run. A ball was added. The cannon was lashed to the mast, and Garcia ran forwards and looked at the ferry which was quarter way across.

'Closer he said. 'We must get closer.'

'We will run aground,' said Skinny. The ship lurched but kept going.

'Now,' Garcia shouted. 'Drop anchor.' The anchor was dropped and the ship swung slowly around, bringing the cannon to bear in the direction of the ferry. Garcia fired the cannon. A plume of water rose near the far bank, nowhere near the ferry. Garcia was loading again and winching the cannon. I thought *hopeless* – the moving ship making it impossible to aim. He fired again. This time, no plume of water. Then I realised he was not firing at the ferry, but the winch holding it, as the ropes pulling the ferry went slack, and the ferry began to drift in our direction. Doyle and the Captain grabbed the loose rope and tried to haul the ferry back but to no avail. The tide drove the ferry into our arms, and their efforts caused us to break out in triumphant laughter. A boat was lowered, and the ferry made fast as we loaded the coffins onto the ship. Before we had finished, Joshua and his men of holy war had arrived back. They chased away the remaining loyalist force and gathered on the bank, shouting wishes for our future, backed up by prayers that their wishes would be fulfilled, and never once using bad language. Only Doyle and the loyalist captain were left on the ferry. Doyle knew there was no point in looking for mercy. Wexford cut the rope holding the ferry, and it began to drift towards the bank where the enraged Joshua waited. Doyle jumped before it reached the bank, preferring the watery death. The captain did not, but he should have; we watched as Joshua and his holy men hacked him to pieces. Joshua, all the time, was staring at the ship; at me, I felt. I turned to James.

'Do you think they are right?' I asked. 'They told me today is not Christmas day.' James pointed at the gold on the deck.

'Does it matter? For us, it is.' Garcia was looking out to sea.

'Where now?' he asked James.

'Home,' said James. Garcia asked as he always did.

'My home?'

'New Ross,' James said, 'then your home.'

'My home,' Garcia did not believe his ears.

'Well, if you don't want to go,' began James. Garcia was gone shouting for more sail.

At New Ross, as supplies for the voyage were loaded, I saddled Sleepy and headed back to the village of widows. As I approached, I could see women and children gathering and chopping firewood, as the cutting wind pulled at my clothing for entry. I rode through the village. They followed me. As I pulled up in front of Mary's cottage she came out, her face flushed.

'You came back,' she said, her eyes shining with something that made me feel uneasy. 'I prayed that you would.' I looked around at the women and children.

'I am not staying,' I said. 'I want ye all to come with me. There is a chance for a new home, a new life. Here there is only poverty and death, for you and your children.'

'I will go with you,' Mary cried.

'You went with him before and shamed us all with your sins.' This came from a young woman whose pretty face

was distorted with bitterness. 'Do you expect us to con-
done your sins by going with ye?' There was a mumbled
agreement, from the others.

'You, Mary,' I asked.

'I cannot leave them,' she said, 'no matter what they
think, they are still my friends and neighbours.' I looked
around at stony faces; I tried, I thought, is not that enough?
I turned Sleepy around, and he walked back through the
village. I took a last look around; no one was following.
Sleepy stopped. I picked up the reins to kick him into a
canter when I noticed he had stopped at the church. The
door stood ajar. A shiver ran up my back, and I knew I
must go in. I dismounted and walked in the door. The
smell of must and candle wax brought me back in time,
and I knew what I had to do. I pushed through the door
behind the altar, a surplice and soutane hung on a peg. In
a dream, I pulled them over my head. When I emerged,
they were all there, kneeling in front of me. My name is Fr
O'Brien. I introduced myself. My cousin was your priest;
it falls upon me to save what's left of his parish. It was easy
for me now as I incanted the Latin, as I had done so often
before. Revoking the promise to a dead priest in Drogheda,
knowing there was no James to blame this time, my soul
was damned forever. They came to me afterwards saying
how ashamed they were of thinking evil of Mary and me.
They would follow me wherever I wanted to bring them.
Mary came to me; her face red.

'I am sorry, Father.'

'Don't be,' I said. 'There is nothing wrong in wanting
a family. Where we are going, I pray you will have that

chance.' I led them to New Ross and up the gangplank, still wearing the priest's garb. They had been waiting for me. Up went the gangplank. The abuse would come later, but now we sailed for Garcia's home; onboard, fifty men at arms, Garcia's crew, Marg and young Cyril and some other wives and girlfriends. At first, the sickness, where we cursed the sea and Garcia in equal measure. Then heaven. Was it a dream, the sun, friendly people? We were soon respected people of property, with no need to rob or kill. Only James' routine remained the same; the training reminding us that soon the dream would be over. Garcia made a replica of his up-the-sleeve dagger; just a piece of steel with a sharp point which hung from the shoulder. The point sat in a small pocket strapped to my wrist. I was pleased with it and used it for many purposes for which it was not designed. The women from Mary's village had, for the most part, formed relationships, and together with Marg were left in charge. At the end of February, we said goodbye and boarded the ship for home. Despite Marg's pleas and my advice that a man with a family should stay, Wexford came with us. As we sailed out of the bay, I asked James, 'Why go back?'

'They will call us soldiers of fortune, thieves, murderous villains,' James answered. 'Still, it will never be said that the Landers of Landers' Hall broke their word of honour to the last great Irish chieftain Owen roe, Neill, and the papal gold was raised to pay an army; an army they will get.' I knew that, but I wanted someone to tell me why we were leaving heaven and going back to hell. New Ross harbour. We were back. You could feel the tension in the air as we disembarked, people looked at us and whispered to each other.

'Form,' James ordered. The men fell into place. 'Present arms.' Muskets held at the ready. 'March'. We marched to our street. Our men were gone. James walked into Skinny's hotel. A strange man was behind the desk.

'Where is Skinny?' James asked.

'Who?' asked the man.

'The owner,' James said.

'The owner is in the gentleman's club,' said the man looking fearful as we gathered around him. 'Skinny in the gentleman's club?' James was puzzled. Garcia had appeared at James' elbow.

'Where is Skinny?' asked Garcia. He reached out and ran his finger down the front of the man's shirt. The material parted and the man looked down as a thin line of blood began to form on his chest. 'I ask you again,' Garcia said, reaching towards him the glint of steel betraying the knife that I had once felt.

'In jail,' the man blurted. 'They are all in jail.'

'For what?' asked James.

'Running a street of disrepute,' the hapless clerk answered as Garcia's finger played with his shirt button. 'The priests went to Ormond and complained, then the soldiers came and closed it down. The gentlemen's club took it over. They run it now.' One of our men ran in.

'The army have sealed off the street,' he shouted. 'We are surrounded.'

THE MONK

'What's happening?' I asked James.

'We will have to find out,' James said grimly, as he led the way to the gentleman's club. They were there looking prosperous but uneasy.

'Where are my men?' was James' first question.

'Helping the people of New Ross,' one answered.

'Why are they not here where I left them?' James asked politely. They looked at each other.

'The priests and the women got together and sent a petition to Ormond. He came and closed the street and left enough men to see it remained closed, and to see you out of town peacefully.'

'We will leave in the morning,' James conceded. 'Now where are my men?'

'I will get them for you,' said the mayor, happy with the way things were going.

'You do that,' James said. 'You have my word we will all leave in the morning.' The mayor departed and returned, leading what appeared to be fifty monks.

'They were made to repent,' offered one of the gentlemen as we began to recognise familiar faces under the cowls. We gaped at them, mouth open.

'Sorry, captain,' said Skinny. 'They overpowered us. They made us work emptying shitholes and cleaning drains. Then they made us pray until we fell asleep, but they would not let us sleep; they started chanting early every morning, and work and prayer were our lot since you left.' His bony face was contorted with passion, and it suddenly struck me he was the nearest to the image of a monk that I carried in my mind that I had ever seen. I burst out laughing. The laughter spread, from soldier to gentleman, as the objects of our humour huddled together in shame. When the laughter subsided, Skinny asked, 'Can we get dressed now?' James looked at him thoughtfully. 'I left you in charge of a street of sin, and I return and find,' he paused, 'monks. You will remain dressed so until we leave in the morning.'

'Where are our horses?' he asked Skinny. Skinny looked uneasy again.

'They took them.'

'Who took them?' asked James.

'Ormond's men,' said Skinny.

'Yes,' said James. 'You stay dressed as monks, you gave more to others than the average monk.' There was a nervous titter. 'And you will have more time to repent when you walk out of here in the morning. But enough tonight; we are all friends. Tonight we will use the street for the last time the way we knew it.' Skinny's face brightened. 'But not the monks,' James added. 'It would not be fitting. Bring out the beer. All of it.' The mayor opened his mouth to say something.

'Surely,' said James, 'the priests do not want that.'

'But all?' the mayor said, looking at his colleagues.

'Yes,' said James, 'they took our business and our horses, the least I can do is give them a headache.' James was studying them. 'It is mine to waste, is it not.'

'Of course,' they agreed after a pause. The bars were emptied, barrels were rolled to the end of the street. I went with them. We broke them open.

'A toast,' I cried, 'to the brave soldiers who liberated a street in New Ross, a street controlled by their Irish allies, while Cromwell's army occupies Wexford just down that road.' Some were looking friendly, looking at the beer, while others looked angry and threatening. 'But tonight, we can be friends.' I changed tack before things got ugly. 'When Cromwell gets here, Ormond will be somewhere else.'

'When Cromwell gets here and asks for our street, you bloody well will give it to him. You give him the whole damned town. But you won't give him the drink belonging to the Irish mercenaries.'

'Why,' I shouted.

'Because we are going to drink it all,' shouted one back.

'Yes,' I said, every drop. They fell on it as all soldiers would. I made my way back to the gentleman's club for my share. They were seated around the tables as I got back, all drinking their favourite; the more expensive, the better. I wondered where to start. Skinny slipped under my elbow.

'Get me a drink,' he whispered.

'Why?' I asked.

'You made fun of me; they all laughed,' he looked hurt. I wondered was he acting or genuine. 'Sorry,' I said. 'You just looked like a real monk.' James was watching.

'You know I could do nothing,' begged Skinny. 'They had a bloody army. We had no chance. They caught us by surprise. I was having a massage; you know, the special shave, warm cloth over face, soft hand, then the hand got hard and urgent, anyway,' he finished. 'I dozed off, you know, the way you do. When I woke, a soldier was standing there with a musket and a smile. I tell you some of them English fellows are not right,' he shuddered.

'That deserves a drink,' I said, looking at James for permission. He shook his head.

'Not while he is wearing the monk's robe.'

'Can I take it off?' begged Skinny.

James said, 'Maybe you can persuade someone to take your place.' Skinny looked around the room; we were laughing at him again as no one was going to. 'Were you warned?' asked James.

'What?' Skinny said.

'Were you warned?' repeated James.

'No,' said Skinny.

'You were not warned,' persisted James. 'Perhaps the robe of shame should be passed on to a gentleman who most certainly would have known.' Skinny looked over to the gentleman's table who was out of earshot. 'Maybe one of

181

them would look more of a monk than you,' prompted James. 'In fact, why don't we have a contest, who is the most like a monk. Bring in five more of your monks.' Skinny appeared within minutes with five very thirsty looking monks. They looked at James and James looked at the gentlemen and nodded. Skinny went first; he tipped his cowl and asked one would he like to swap his clothes for the habit so that he, Skinny, could avail of the free drink. The gentleman looked him up and down then turned his back, picked up his mug, and resumed the conversation. Skinny looked at James. James nodded. Skinny brought both hands joined together down on the gentleman's neck. The head hit the table, bits of the jug flew; he would need stitches. The gentlemen were up and heading for the door. James shook his head. The door was blocked.

'What did you do that for, Skinny?' James asked.

'What?' Skinny went.

'All you had to do was ask nicely. Now ask again.' Skinny was about to ask, but the man was already undressing.

'Sorry,' said James 'as I have forbidden anyone wearing the habit from joining our party. You can see why he resorted to violence. Why not humour them?' They quickly undressed and donned the habit. Skinny donned the gentleman's clothes. I erupted with laughter again.

'What?' asked Skinny.

'Good monk, bad gentleman!' explained.

'Oh,' he said, looking at me as he weighed our friendship.

'Now, Skinny,' said James, looking at the lined up gentlemen, 'which do you think is the best monk. Remember you have to judge them right, Skinny. You looked like a monk, but you are not; you see, it has more to do with truthfulness. Nothing happens in this town they don't know about. Ask why were you not warned.'

'Why?' Skinny asked, as he went nose to nose with the first in line.

'People would have been killed,' he answered fearfully.

James pointed out, 'That sounds like the answer of a good and truthful monk, but a lie. Garcia,' James called. 'Mark that man with 'l' for liar.' Garcia flicked his wrist down and sideways. James said, 'Now ask the next one.'

'Why were we not warned?' The one Garcia had marked let out a scream as he noticed blood running down his habit. The line of monks began to look uneasy.

'Some of your men would have got hurt defending the street,' the next one said.

'Liar,' James concluded. 'You regard my men as dirt; mark him.' Garcia moved forwards; this one had to be held. Skinny was getting interested as he moved on. He was smiling now; the kind of smile you do not want to see in front of you asking 'why?'

'The property. We did not want to see your property damaged.'

'Lie,' was James' verdict. 'You knew we were moving on.' He had to be held and squealed like a pig. Skinny moved on.

'Why?' The next one was frightened. His eyes darted everywhere, looking for a way out.

'We each get the property we sold you back for nothing.'

'Lie,' James concluded, 'but the truth creeps closer.'

Garcia asked, 'Can I write the full word? This is getting boring.'

'Give that one 't' for truth.' The next one was the mayor.

'Why?' asked Skinny, who had been given drink and did not want the fun to end.

'Tell him the truth,' James advised, 'or it will be a long night for you all.'

'Your men would have defended the street, property would be damaged, and your men would have hidden the takings of the business,' the mayor said.

'At last,' James said, 'we have found a truthful monk.'

LEAVING
NEW ROSS

James sent more drink to the soldiers. Garcia broke into his shop and the monks smuggled the arms to the Gentleman's club and loaded four to each man. By morning, clothing shops had been raided by the monks. Some, late to make their choices, looked like brothel keepers, while the brothel keepers looked like gents. They had one thing in common – pistols were stuck into every belt, every garish duplet, every boot. As dawn broke, James stood before us.

'Today, we leave New Ross. We leave the street. We leave the gentlemen dead. We leave everyone who stands armed in our way dead. We leave as planned, half of us; when we are passing by them at the end of the street, we will open fire. The soldiers at the top of the street will come to their assistance. You, the remaining fifty, will let them pass into a crossfire. Then we will take back our horses. Let this be a lesson to us – we cannot trust anyone outside of ourselves.' The gentlemen who were bound and gagged were mumbling and struggling as they heard their death sentence. 'Kill them quietly,' James ordered. The mumbling got desperate. 'Wait,' James said. 'They may want to leave notes for their loved ones. Give them pen and ink.' The mumbling got worse.

'I think the mayor wants to say something,' I ventured. James relented.

'Kill him if he tries to scream.' I removed the gag as Garcia stood beside me, picking his nails with his knife. The mayor tried to talk, but no words came out.

'Go ahead,' I said to Garcia; the words came then.

'It was not the priests that closed the street. His nephew was an officer in Ormond's army. We made a deal. They wanted the horses. We would have the takings and the street back. The takings are still here in the cellar. I will ask that the horses be returned.' James sighed.

'But you can't ask. They would be warned. You and your friends will leave with us and see what happens when trust is broken.' Skinny led off, dwarfed by a large drum. The gentlemen were next, dressed as monks, tied to a long pole; their habit tied over their heads to conceal their gags. James nodded and Skinny brought the drumsticks down, his head turned sideways to hear the deafening noise. Heads appeared. Soldiers came out to see the gentlemen naked under the pole trying to run in different directions. Soldiers at the end of the street came out, then called others; soon, the end of the street was lined with soldiers as others at the top of the street came out to see what the noise was. As James drew level with the soldiers he rose his hand. The drum went silent. 'You should not have come into my street.' They looked at him, puzzled; some of them drunk, some half-dressed. James dropped his hand. The surprised soldiers had no chance, as musket and pistols discharged into them at pointblank range. Some ran back indoors to arm themselves; they were shot or surrendered as James and his men took cover in the houses. The soldiers at the top of the street armed themselves and came running down the street to help their stricken comrades. Nothing remained in the street but the dead and the naked gentlemen. They were trying to run, but not easy when you can't see and tied to a pole. They ran into walls and tripped over bodies. Their soldiers killed them. They were the only targets left in the street, except themselves. We who had stayed in the club opened fire on their rear; caught between James and us, they began to fall, until an officer called for quarter. James spoke to him of robbers and horse thieves and regret that their actions had led to bloodshed. With his leave, we would collect our horses and leave without further friction between allies such as us. They gave us back our horses. We freed our captives, mounted our horses and rode from our street. The rain cascaded down, washing the blood into the gutters as we passed. We were home.

WATERFORD

The people we passed were starving. Most were women and children. The men who cared little for kings or parliament enlisted by the priest's promises of blessings and eternal life. They watched as we passed, their eyes blank. They did not beg; the begging would come later. Waterford lay before us. In the bay, we could see Garcia's ship. We elbowed through the crowd that had gathered on the road leading into the town. People were pleading for entry, as a troop led by a portly sergeant blocked their way.

'What's the problem?' inquired James.

'Not enough food.'

'Too much, I would have thought,' said Wexford, eying the sergeant up and down. The sergeant flushed.

'Not enough food,' he repeated, 'not for them.' He indicated the sorry-looking women and children. 'Not for every beggar on horseback trying to make like an army.' His eyes locked with Wexford.

'Quite right,' said James. He dismounted, and walked towards the sergeant who backed away. James put his arm around his shoulder and led him away, whispering. They stood looking out to sea. The sergeant went to the gate, had a whispered conversation with an officer. They beckoned James through; we saw them take a boat to Garcia's ship. The boat returned to the quay, the gates opened. We rode in. We were again confronted. This time, the portly sergeant threw his arm around the officer and whispered, and we were in Waterford. We unloaded the ship's cargo onto boats; some for the officers and Waterford. The bulk of the supplies were for Clonmel. Those were transferred to flat-bottomed sailing ships for the journey up the river to Carrick-on-Suir, there to be transferred to barges for the final leg of the journey.

'We will rest here a while,' James announced. Jars of wine were sent with the compliments of James Landers. Soon, he was swanning around with the nobility while telling us to relax and discuss all of the cruelties we had witnessed; of this, he was insistent. I soon had a rapt audience, as rum and beer loosened my brain and dragged my memory back to things I had tried to forget. As tears flowed freely from my eyes, few that heard my story doubted; but one said, 'The priest told us at Mass that when Cromwell's men went to shoot the priests, their pistols would not fire.' 'If that is true,' I countered, 'God did them a great disservice,' launching into the story of how the priests in Drogheda and Wexford died. There were gasps of horror; soon, the whole town was talking about us. We ate and dined well.

Garcia left the ship in Skinny's hands and led the flotilla of hired boats up the Suir. We followed on land, keeping them in sight as much as we could. The blight of war had not spread here but walked with us; the pitiful undernourished had despaired of entry to Waterford and were heading inland.

'There,' said James, 'go the perfect killing machine, bringing with them hunger and disease. Those kind enough to share with them will join them in their march of death. Damn them,' James said. 'damn their king, damn their parliament, damn them all to hell.' I saw tears in his eyes; it worried me, as we all knew, as he did, the food in the boats would keep them alive longer, but without it, we would share the same end. We rode by them, avoiding their eyes, as the shame of not helping spread through us. Carrick-on-Suir. Wine and fruit were distributed again to town rulers. We men spent freely and told our tales of horror, while at the same time our numbers swelled as it had in Waterford. Young men looked at us in awe. We were tanned and well-fed with coins to spare. They wanted to be like us, whereas I would have given all to be like them again. James assured the powers that be that his ship would supply as much food as possible through Waterford, and they should not take up arms, as they would struggle to feed the stricken population who were already entering the town.

I asked why we were frightening people and advising against taking part in the war in Carrick and Waterford. He said, 'We need the Suir to bring in food. If we come back this way, we will need live friends, not dead heroes. I hope they listen to us.' We loaded the food onto barges with horses attached to pull them to Clonmel. We followed, keeping the barges in sight. Outside Carrick stood a stone fortress, gates closed with no sign of life, but as we passed a plume of smoke billowed from the tower. James looked uneasy. He raised a hand, bringing the troop to a halt.

'We will scout ahead,' he looked at Wexford. 'Take command,' and beckoned me to come with him. I smirked at Wexford as I passed.

'Stay safe now,' I jeered. Soon we came to a castle surrounded by a small village; again, no sign of life; again, smoke from a turret.

'We are being watched,' said James, 'but why?'

'We could ask,' I pointed out.

'Why not?' James said. We rode within hailing distance of the castle. James called out that Landers of Landers' Hall desired entry. His voice echoed off the walls. There was no other sound. We waited. The barges came into view on the river below. Sleepy was getting restless; he started snorting and dancing, taking me in a complete circle.

'James,' I said, my voice came out in a whisper. 'James,' I repeated, this time a lot louder. He looked around. Lined up a hundred yards away, Roundheads. The mounted ones in front had already drawn swords and broke into a gallop, while the foot soldiers trotted behind. For once, getting back to the oaf called Wexford was much desired, but he was gone. Then James' horse went down, sending him crashing to the ground. The lead Roundhead was bearing down on James when Sleepy crashed into him, but the abrupt stop sent me flying over his head. I landed beside the motionless James, quickly covering his body with mine. I braced for the feel of a sword thrust that did not come. The horses past by and over us, then came the foot soldiers, then more horses. I covered my head as they flew by, grunting as the odd hoof slammed into my body. Dead bodies lay around me now. Dazed, I looked up. The Roundhead foot soldiers and the mounted ones were in a desperate group, fighting for their lives, while soldiers I had not seen before were picking them off at will; fighting with them was Wexford and our men.

THE HERALD

Then he saw me, and walked over to me, leaving the slaughter behind.

'Are you just going to lie there?' he asked, in that mocking voice I hated. I stood up. James groaned as I rose for a moment. I saw concern on Wexford's face. 'When ye left, I hailed the castle again. They told us there were Roundhead troops on the way. That was what the signals meant. We caught them in a trap. It is almost over.' James sat up. He looked blankly around. The Roundhead officer was being held between two strange soldiers, while another was asking him questions. He pointed towards the river. They had spies. Their job was to cut off supplies to Clonmel. James was on his feet. He staggered.

'I need to know where I am. River,' he said, pointing at the river. 'Trees,' pointing at the trees. 'Mountains,' he spun around, indicating the mountains. 'Men,' he said, looking at the Roundhead officer.

'No, enemy,' said Wexford patiently. James looked around. 'Poachers, woodsmen'.

'No, soldiers,' Wexford said worriedly, noticing the trickle of blood coming from James' head. The soldier questioning the Roundhead ran him through.

'No,' said James sadly, going to the stricken officer and gently lifting him. 'You cut his tunic, and it is all stained.' He took the tunic off and stuck his finger through the hole and wiggled his finger. 'I never learned to sew,' he confided, his vacant eyes looking reproachfully at us.

'I had an uncle who went like that,' someone behind me said as we gathered around him.

'Nor wash, nor iron,' James continued.

'I have a wife like that,' someone said. No one laughed. We had a leader who wanted to be a housewife.

'Well, get me one,' James said patiently.

'One what?' I asked to humour him.

'A wife that can,' he said.

'They all can,' I said.

'Not mine,' someone said behind me unhelpfully.

'Will getting married not wait until after the war?' I asked.

'Who is getting married?' James asked.

'You are,' we chorused to humour him.

'Get me someone to wash and iron this uniform, you pack of idiots,' he added; the old James was back. We thanked our saviours who told us they were on their way to Kilkenny to defend the town. Then, to my annoyance, thanked Wexford for his help.

'What now?' I asked James.

'Did I not I tell you? We need men who know the rivers, the woods and the mountains, don't you ever listen?' James was dazzling; his buttons gleamed, his boots shone, the horses' bridle and saddle gleamed. They had salvaged another uniform for me, but I was not happy as it had no gold braid and very ordinary buttons. I set off after him leaving Wexford and our men to follow us. We went, as James put it, to 'take castles'. The first thing we did when out of sight was construct a flag, a white one, which suited me, as I had seen first-hand what happened to people who followed coloured ones. I just hoped we would not meet anyone like ourselves who might ignore it. We went from castle to castle, prancing our horses up and down in front of them. James read a prepared speech which, if you ignored the flowery text, stated if resistance was offered to the parliament forces, all within would be slaughtered. We arrived at a well-walled town called Fethard. The name 'Cromwell' was enough to open their gates for us. We rode in; little children who played in the street were grabbed and took indoors, women crossed themselves as we passed, the church door was shut. The mayor and his clerk rode with us to the town hall. We tied the horses; a table laden with food and drink awaited us. We sat. I grabbed a leg of lamb and sunk my teeth into it. James looked on me with disdain. I stopped in mid-chew. I thought, he is not going to pull the grace before meals trick on me again. Instead, still looking at me, he said, 'We are not all savages you know.' I looked from him to the faces of the mayor and his clerk. 'We have thousands of people like this one,' James continued, still looking at me, 'who only live to kill, eat and fornicate. We have thousands more who wish to kill all who do not share their views on the good book. I, on the other hand, wish only for all lands within five miles of Fethard. All who live here can serve me well; for this, I will stand between you and the ravenous hordes who approach as we speak; but what do I see here?' I looked at the leg of lamb. What more did he want? I thought. Maybe beef? 'Ingratitude,' he thundered. 'Why do we dine alone? Where is my welcome?' The mayor rushed out; soon, music played. The square was full of people. We mingled like lords. James seemed intent on organising his fictional estate, awarding jobs of mucking out stables and dung spreading at random. Some were not impressed, and I caught some un-servant like looks directed at him behind his back. I wished he would stop. I was enjoying being the savage described, but any chance of fornication was unlikely, as any female I approached with the courage of drink were whisked away by their menfolk. Before we left, James wrote a letter for the mayor, detailing in glowing terms how Fethard was a friend of the parliament, and no harm should befall it or its people. I had my problems. My head ached with every step Sleepy took. We came back to the Suir again; we had completed a circle. There before us was a castle. We decided to do our act. James went into his pompous officer routine, while I played a sullen hungover soldier with plain buttons. The gates opened, and six un-couth fellows on horseback charged out, shouting what we could do with our terms, and they would help by shoving their swords up after them. We fled back to Wexford and his army, and it was an army. They quickly surrounded our pursuers, who could have come to a bad end but for James shouting 'no-no-no'.

'Am I your mother?' sneered Wexford at me, as he turned to James.

'It was as you,said Wexford, 'told James as we followed you; those who wished to fight enlisted with the promise of coins and food.' Our pursuers invited us to join them for a meal in the castle, relieved as they were that we were friends. Poulakerry castle it was called. There we dined on salmon and mutton, and washed it down with wine we brought from the barge. We met the wife of the lord of the castle. She held a baby in one hand and talked to a small boy who followed her everywhere holding a pup. James rubbed the pup's head and asked the boy's name. Brian was the answer.

'And the dog?' prompted James.

'Pup,' Brian said.

'Named after your brother,' Wexford remarked to James.

'Looks like you now, but he will grow out of it, unlike you,' I retorted. James shook his head in despair. The host regaled us of his family history and his pride in the castle, and Cromwell and his ungodly hordes would enter it over his dead body. Our hostess laid down the baby in its cot and had sat behind a harp and began to sing. All went quiet, her eyes had closed, and you knew she had left for the place in her song, where love and peace reigned. When it was over, she waited for the last notes to fade, before opening her eyes. She looked from one to the other of us. Tears were in her eyes. She said nothing, gathered her children and left us.

CLONMEL

As the men gathered to leave, James and I went to the castle to thank our hosts. They were there, a family; she, dark and beautiful, holding the baby while the boy held her leg in one hand and the pup in the other; the lord, like he was posing for a portrait, all pride and bravado. James said, 'We will take our leave. Thank you for your hospitality. We have become unused to kindness and good company. I would ask to perform one task to thank you; I would be honoured to escort your family to Clonmel, and rest assured I would treat them as I would my own.' James was looking at our host, whose face had darkened. But it was she who answered.

'My place is by my husband's side.'

'What of them?' James asked, indicating the children.

'Their place is with their mother,' she answered.

'We will take our leave then,' said James. He swung his horse abruptly and was gone, leaving me looking at the family.

'He worries,' I explained, 'about people,' I added vaguely.

'Tell him thanks,' it was our hostess. I gathered the reins.

'I have seen things,' I said. 'You should come.' They did not answer, just waited for me to leave. When I looked back, they were gone. Clonmel lay before us, a walled town with the river guarding one side, set in a rich fertile valley beneath well-wooded mountains. The barges pulled up at the riverside as we announced ourselves as Landers of Landers' Hall, sent by Owen Roe O'Neill to defend Clonmel against the parliament and Oliver Cromwell. The gates swung open. We had come to the end of our journey.

Having washed and shaved in Poulakerry, James and I went for a tour of the town, followed by a group of our men. From the beginning, it became clear that our presence was tolerated only on the basis of our fighting ability, as all respectable people turned away as we approached. Any damsel who chanced a smile in our direction was whisked away, and doors banged. We were only welcome at a house where a bevy of crones shouted prices for services, most of which I had never heard of. I hoped we would never get that desperate, but noticed that some of our men already had. We approached a large building with 'town hall' written over it. We heard music. James went in, and I followed. The officers of the garrison were having a ball. The officers were dressed in their ceremonial uniforms, but we were not looking at them. We were looking at the women. For the first time, I realised why men could kill for love instead of land, food or money. The music suddenly stopped at the raised hand of a tall, fair-haired man in a most impressive uniform, with a dazzling shine on his boots, who strode in our direction to welcome us, I thought. 'Get out,' he said to James. 'Get out.' James was not listening; he was looking at the woman the peacock had been dancing with, oblivious of all but her.

'Good evening,' said James. 'I would like the honour of the next dance.'

'I would be delighted, sir,' she said. The officer went red with temper.

'Get out, scum, or I will have you thrown out,' he ranted.

'At the party in the square tonight at ten, I will claim that pleasure,' said James. It was my turn to ignore the officer as I jumped to confirm the party, brushing him aside as I asked James, 'Permission to gather a band?'

'You may,' said James, still smiling at the woman. The garrison leader slapped me angrily on the back. I turned. We were nose to nose.

'You cannot play in my band,' I said. He was about to jump back to shout some orders to his men, who were trying not to look amused, but discovered I had his belt in my hand.

'You are not invited,' I said, leaning over so his body bent to avoid our noses, making contact as I let Garcia's dagger prick his stomach. 'Do you understand?' I asked. I released his belt; he jumped back. I stood there empty handed; before he regained his voice, we were gone. James went to arrange food and drink for the party, while I toured the town, recruiting musicians, all bar drummers, as I had seen Skinny in New Ross and knew I was better. Tables were robbed from houses and food piled high as our army gathered in the square. Then the band struck up with a thunderous roar of drums, of which I was the proud producer. Nobody danced; there were no women. Then a door opened, and a woman walked up the street; the army parted to let her through, as it did for James. They met in the middle of the circle of men and, without a word spoken, began to dance. They danced as if nobody else existed in that time and space except themselves. They floated around the square, bodies twining and swirling, while all the time their eyes never left the others. Something crashed into my ear; it was the accordion man's elbow. I moved my head to one side. Then I saw other doors opening as people poured into the square. Our army turned into rabble as they bumped and pushed each other to be first to get to the women. James and partner danced on, oblivious of the chaos around them. Something crashed into my skull; it was a lump of brass on an instrument I had not seen before. Then I saw the fiddler's bow heading for my eye. I jerked my head away and was hit again by the accordion man's elbow; at this stage, I decided to give a chance to a fellow standing nearby with drumsticks who had been watching me in amazement. I had to admit he was not so bad, if a trifle monotonous for my taste.

A voice said, 'All the women are blaming you for their sore toes.' I turned to say something scathing about women who could not follow a beat, only to see a vision of beauty. She was as tall as myself and dark as myself, but in no other way similar.

'But I thought you were good,' she finished. My brain stopped working, the angry retort I had been about to voice got mixed up with 'thanks' and 'you are beautiful', and emerged in a meaningless babble. My mouth stayed open in the hope that it would say something witty and meaningful, but nothing came out.

'Would you like to dance?' she asked; and getting no answer, asked, 'Are you dumb?'

'Yes,' I said.

'Yes you are dumb, or yes you will dance?' she asked, but she was smiling.

'Both,' I said, the blood that was making my face red also getting my brain working, and I managed a smile.

We danced. I remembered now with gratitude Martha's lessons, dancing around the kitchen; a source of embarrassment then, but now a lifesaver. We merged; she floated, and I somehow kept up.

'Relax,' she said into my ear. I did and found it came easy to me. 'See,' she whispered, 'how we blend?' Her body brushed mine, making me conscious of the effect her nearness was having on my body. Then, I saw the garrison leader. He was watching from the wings. The dance took me away; when I came back into sight, he was talking to another officer. They were both peering into the crowd of dancers. I was whirled away again, my sex becoming more and more a problem. Then I saw Wexford talking to the officer. They were both looking into the crowd. I followed their eyes to James. I danced away; my problem had disappeared. 'Am I boring you?' she asked. I looked at her sharply, her eyes were wide and innocent.

'No,' I said, 'but I think duty calls.'

'Are you going to walk me home?' she asked. 'We hear stories here of soldiers who take what they want. Would you expose me to such peril?'

'Yes, I will,' said.

'You will expose me to peril, or you will walk me home?' she asked. There was something wrong. A small voice inside my head was telling me. Then she smiled at me, and we walked from the square. People stared at us, but quickly looked away when I looked back. The little voice came back. She walked head high, looking straight ahead as she went through her door. I turned to leave. 'Do you not want to see me again?' she asked.

'Yes,' I said.

'What's wrong with now?' her voice was husky and I went inside. We kissed. I felt the power running through me, and there was no stopping now. We became as two animals, clothes discarded as we loved our way to the bedroom. I took her violently as her nails raked down my back. When it was over for me, she persisted; her tongue licking my nipples – useless things until she touched them. Her tongue travelled down my body; my mind said 'you are flogging a dead horse,' but my body responded. She straddled me, then gently moving back and forwards and whispering something to herself in a kind of moan. The alarm bells that had tinkled in my mind all evening became lost in the passion of the moment; as she climaxed, her maniac eyes looked into my ecstatic ones. But as I came, my mind had deciphered what she was saying. It was 'kill him for me, kill him for me.' A chill ran up my backbone. I was cold, calculating and sexless.

'Who,' I asked 'do you want killed?' She looked at me, her eyes normal and beautiful and innocent and said:

'The garrison leader'.

'Why?' I asked, my transition from total happiness to shock dictating my questions.

'Because if you don't, he will kill you.'

'Why?' I asked, 'would he want to kill me?'

'Well,' she said, 'you made him look small in front of his friends, and you have just been in bed with his woman.' My mind recoiled in horror. I pulled on my breeches; my hand fumbled in my pocket and threw her a few coins.

'Whores are paid in coins, not in blood.' Her eyes showed hurt and humiliation.

'But you don't understand. I saved you. You would be with them in the town hall, and you are condemned to death. The mayor's wife told me if I saved you, you would leave and take me with you.'

'My brother is there,' I screamed. I grabbed sabre and dagger and ran. I could hear her shouting after me.

'I did not know. I didn't know.' Our men were standing in groups around the square.

'To me,' I screamed. 'To me', as I ran for the town hall. I was glad now of the training, as I heard them running behind me; then, I rounded the corner.

TO DIE IN CLONMEL

James and Wexford walked the cobbled street to the town hall. There they sat; the great and good of the town presided over by the mayor. Three chairs stood empty at the end of the table. The mayor indicated the empty chairs.

'Shall we wait for your brother?' the mayor asked.

'He had a pressing engagement elsewhere,' James said. The mayor glanced towards the garrison commander, who growled.

'Get on with it.' The mayor cleared his throat.

'We have here seated around this table, Fr Casey, who represents Bishop Watkins and the Holy See, the garrison leader Captain Rossiter, who represents His Majesty. We have others who have entered into an arrangement to defend Clonmel for monetary reasons or perhaps the restoration of former positions.' The mayor continued. 'I, on the other hand, represent the citizens of this town. Together we face the greatest threat to our faith and way of life we are ever likely to encounter. I ask that the decisions taken here tonight keep the welfare of the people of this town in mind. I now call on Fr Casey to lead us in prayer.' Fr Casey stood; a florid-faced man with receding hair. The priest proclaimed that soon outside the gates of Clonmel would come the hordes of evil, the representatives of satan himself. The gates should be closed against him. Those that contemplate otherwise would join them in eternal damnation in the flames of hell.' His face had gone red, spittle flew from his mouth. He sat abruptly. Wexford leaned over and whispered to James.

'I know a man called Joshua would be impressed by that.' The garrison leader was next.

'I,' he paused for effect, 'represent his most gracious Majesty, King Charles. It will be my privilege to defend the walls of Clonmel against those that would deny my king his God-given right to rule his subjects. Those that stand with me will reap the rewards when His Majesty is victorious.' He looked around, bestowing a gracious smile upon the gathering. 'All bearing arms shall answer to me in defence of this town.' The mayor looked at James.

'My men fight on my orders only. I will pay them. I will feed them. You, mayor, what of your people? His King, will he feed the women and children? Will the church put food on your table? No, not in this life. Get your people out of this town, mayor,' James finished. The mayor looked from one face to another in search of reassurance; none came.

He shuffled some papers, rose to his feet and was about to speak when the garrison commander said, 'That will be all, mayor.' The mayor got to his feet and left with his committee. The garrison leader put it in words; 'Whose side are you on, frightening the townspeople like that?'

'They need to know what may befall them should they stay,' James pointed out.

'They will be safe in the bosom of our holy mother, the church,' the priest said.

'I feed twelve hundred soldiers,' the garrison leader added.

'I have four hundred men and one hundred horses,' said James. 'Which of you undertake to provide food for the townspeople?' They looked at each other.

'Everyone will share food and hardship equally,' the priest said.

'Well not me,' James said. Fr Casey was on his feet.

'What else could we expect from one such as you, a thief and a murderer?' Something had crept into the room, and Wexford sat up in his chair. His hand fell to the butt of his pistol. The priest continued. 'A man who desecrated the altar of God, set free a crew of heathen pirates, murdered Captain Blount, stole a shipment of gold on route for the papal army, and killed fifty of Lord Ormond's men in a dispute over a brothel.'

'Horses,' James corrected. 'Horses'. The garrison leader was staring at James.

'So you do not deny it?

'I promised Owen Roe O'Neill I would gather men to defend Clonmel. He knew who I was and what I was, he trusted me to honour my commitment, and I trust him to honour his.' The garrison leader stood.

'Fr Casey has listed the charges against you, and as you have admitted them, it only remains to carry out the sentence of death. You have brought four hundred men here. I thank you for that. We will leave you the only man you will need – your priest.' Wexford went to rise; James stopped him.

'Very wise,' the garrison commander said. 'Look outside. You have fifteen minutes with your priest. If you don't come out, they will come in.' Fr Casey did not look happy. Wexford was walking towards him; his intention obvious.

'Leave him,' James ordered.

'The bishop gave me a sealed letter for the garrison leader,' the priest explained. The priest looked fearfully at the scowling Wexford.

'Would you like to hear my confession?' Wexford asked menacingly.

'We only have ten minutes,' the priest replied.

'Then we should say a prayer,' James suggested. 'Wexford join us in a prayer.' Wexford looked puzzled. The priest began.

'We pray to God to deliver us from sin,' and my brother James interrupted, 'to deliver us from evil.'

'Amen,' Wexford finished. They both laughed

Outside, the soldiers wondered at the men who could laugh in the face of death. When the time came to leave, James told Wexford to leave your weapons.

'They will not help us now, only hasten our death. Lead us in prayer.' The priest started to pray, and James and Wexford followed him out the door.

James and Wexford were being led towards the river when we hit them. I saw the weapons rise, but I was upon them. The sabre went through the first and wrenched from my hand, then something hit me. I lashed out and the dagger bit and I was through. I tried to turn but my legs tangled and I went down. Wexford bent over me.

'You took your time,' he accused, but he was looking at my side. Our army was around us now, mean and angry, they carried me between them as James shouted, 'Clear the north street. Everyone out.' I was laid on a bed, warm from someone's body, as all the residents were forced out.

Then she came; her and a grey-haired woman. They washed me. The older woman put some evil smelling balm on my side and wrapped me in bandages round and round. Then the darkness. The crone sat astride me, toothless mouth, cackling 'kill him for me, kill him for me.' Green bile oozed from her mouth into mine. I tried to spit it out. She vomited on my head, but it was cold and comfortable. I could see her eyes. They were concerned. Then they changed and the crone came back. 'Kill him for me, kill him for me.' Peace. I could see a man on a bed as I floated over him. I wanted to float away in peace. Then I heard my voice saying, 'Killed in an alley in Clonmel, your epitaph.' I went back, and the body that was mine open its eyes and she was there, the woman I had learned to love and hate all in one night, looking at me in relief as well she might, as the contract she had signed with her body might yet be honoured. I turned my face to the wall. After a while, she left. The grey-haired woman still came next day and fed me soup. She said she could get me back to health, but could do nothing for my meanness. Still she came every day. After a week, I got to walk; the pain from my knitting ribs helped by the bandages that swaddled me. One day, my nurse brought her to me; the woman who had stolen my heart and destroyed it all in one night.

'I would have come sooner,' she said.

'But she could not walk,' interrupted my nurse. I could see the bruises on her face and we stared at one another, strangers; yet we knew nothing would ever replace what was between us. We talked about nothing, then she said, 'I must go. He will be back soon.'

'If I leave here alive, will you come with me?' I asked.

'Yes,' she said. 'I will go with you.' Then she smiled a sad smile, as one does when they wish for something that will never happen, and was gone.

James and Wexford had been busy. The street now had another gate leading to the river. It was guarded, as was the north gate facing towards Fethard. The windows and doors were also strengthened. The mayor came with his wife, who I was surprised to find was my nurse. They pleaded for the return of the houses. He was told curtly the street would be defended from attackers from inside or outside the walls. An uneasy peace was agreed within the town. News came. Waterford, Fethard, Carrick and Callan had taken terms and were in enemy hands. Food became scarce within the town. The garrison leader proclaimed that Kilkenny would hold and His Majesty's forces would drive off the attackers.

Skinny was told no food was to pass Carrick. The net was tightening. The clatter of horseshoes on the cobbles woke me. I made my painful way to the door. James was at the head of a hundred horses with bags of provisions hanging from the saddles. He turned to me.

'Wexford is in command here now.' He waited for an argument; none came. He picked up a horn that hung from his saddle and blew into it. I reached up to cover my ears. The movement sent pain shooting through my body. 'When you here this horn again, open those gates. We will be coming back in. That is your task.'

'Yes,' I said sourly. 'Wexford commands, and I open gates.' He looked at me, shook his head sadly, and rode out the gate at the head of his men. Garcia rode beside him. 'Take care,' I called after him, but the gates had already closed behind him.

THE KING OF CLONMEL

The garrison leader surveyed his kingdom. The town of Clonmel was a far cry from what a man of his breeding was entitled to rule. His father was in line for the throne of England, and he had sent his son to this sodden godforsaken land. His mother, a courtesan and long-term mistress of his father, had presented him to his father as a young boy. His father, overweight, with the ravaged face of a man who had spent his life in pursuit of a good time, had left the good times behind him.

'This is your son,' she said. I expect you to do right by him. His Lordship had regarded the boy with bloodshot eyes.

'My son, you say.' His eyebrows rose in derision.

'Yes,' she said. 'Your son'.

'Am I to believe you were so overcome by my last visit you became celibate?' he retorted, sarcasm dripping from his voice.

'Yes,' she said. 'On your last visit you gave me a son and made me celibate. You gave me the pox.' He stared at the woman for a moment weighing up her statement. Then he reached into his desk, took a purse from it and left it in front of the mother.

'You will be looked after,' he said. The woman smiled, took the purse in one hand and the child's hand in the other, and turned for the door. 'Leave the boy,' the man said. The mother dropped the boy's hand without breaking stride and vanished from his life. The child did not cry; he had been left alone before. The man pulled a rope hanging from the ceiling. A bell rang in the distance. A man appeared. 'This is my son. See he gets everything he needs.'

Twenty years later, he was in Clonmel. All because he had killed a fellow who had insulted him, mocking him and calling him a bastard in front of his friends. He had followed the fellow out of the club and knifed him to death in an alley. The fellow was well connected and respected. His father called him into his den.

'My name cannot protect you. This time, you have gone too far. I have property in Ireland. It is best you go there.' Then came the damned war. His father sent soldiers; his hopes of a return to England dashed.

As his father's representative, he attended town council meetings. That was where he saw her first, the newly-wed wife of a tradesman who had come to the meeting to offer his services. He pursued her relentlessly. She seemed amused at first, laughing off his advances. Then one day finding her alone he grabbed her and tried to kiss her. She gave him an open-handed stinging slap across the cheek.

'For shame, sir,' she said. 'I am a married woman.' She ran away. He could not follow; he was shaking with desire. No woman had ever done that to him before. Before morning, she was a widow; her husband dragged from the river two weeks later. When she tried to leave the town, his men brought her back. Soon she came to him as he knew she would. She asked to be allowed to leave. He outlined the advantages of staying in his company. She refused.

'I had your husband killed,' he said. She had come prepared. A knife flashed; he disarmed her easily; again, the passion he had never known. This time he would not let her run away.

In Clonmel, he was not given everything he needed. He took it. Nothing in his past had prepared him for the feelings that now beset him. He became as much a prisoner as she. Then came the mercenaries. They seemed wild and undisciplined. It should have been a simple matter; execute the warrant, remove the leaders, recruit his followers, and send them to Irishtown with the rest of the rabble. She had scuppered his plans by removing the thug who had prodded him at the ball. Now they were embedded in a street in his town. His mind in turmoil with a mixture of jealousy and rage. Had she given willingly what he had to take? Sooner or later, he would get her back. What then? His dwelt on the thought. Soon he felt better.

POULAKERRY

J ames rode out of Clonmel at the head of a hundred horses. The jeers of the garrison soldiers followed them.

'They don't think we are coming back,' observed Garcia. James said nothing; we headed for Slievenamon, guided by the local recruits. There in a clearing, we made camp. Sentries were posted and local recruits were sent back to their towns and villages with orders to report back on anything of importance. In the days that followed, James and Garcia would climb Carrigloe rock, where a view of the valley from Callan to Clonmel could be seen through Garcia's telescope. Word came back from the scout soldiers massing in Carrick, Cahir and Fethard, and some had taken over Duff Hill castle, with little resistance. The noose was tightening on Clonmel. Then it started; a force of around 200 men on foot with a supply wagon left Carrick. We watched from our perch as they called for the surrender of Poulakerry.

They got the same answer as James had got, and set up camp in front of the castle. A rider broke from the rear of the castle and rode for Clonmel. No attempt was made to stop him. James called for his local woodsman.

'If we move by night, how close can we get to Poulakerry without been seen?'

'I will get you within a half mile tonight, with no moon,' he assured James.

'Then we move tonight.' The morning broke and we could see the castle plainly, and the Roundhead camp where the soldiers went about their business in a carefree way; the smell of cooking blown by the wind, teasing us as we watched. The men watched James for a signal to attack, but James, with Garcia by his side, just watched. Garcia broke first.

'What are we waiting for?' he inquired.

'To find out what kind of foe we are dealing with,' said James.

'Well he can't be that good. He sends 200 men into enemy held land when he should have sent 1,000.'

'That bad or that good?' mused James. A plume of smoke arose from Duff Hill castle. 'Ah,' said James. 'It begins.' The camp had also seen it and dropped everything and began to trot back in the direction of Carrick. We could feel it, the tremor in the ground; horses, lots of them. They swept past our position, garrison troops from Clonmel, around 400, only to be confronted by twice that number riding out of Carrick. The Clonmel cavalry passed by us in disarray, as a troop out of Fethard cut them off from Clonmel. The din of battle receded into the distance.

'Well,' James said to Garcia grimly. 'he is that good.' The 200 Roundheads had come back to Poulakerry and were joined by the returning cavalry. The smell of cooking again filled the air. We heard them before we saw them; the grind of steel rims against the stony road; and as they hove into view, our hearts sank – cannon. 'He is good, and wastes no time,' James noted. Two mounted Roundheads approached the castle and called out for its surrender. 'He will surrender the castle,' said James. 'He must have seen the cannon; he has a wife and two children in there, he must.' A shot rang out, and the Roundheads wheeled their horses. 'The fool,' James cried out, but the roar of the cannon drowned it out. The Roundheads had formed a rough line behind the cannon and observed the ball cut a furrow through the ground in front of the castle door. The gunner had a word with his helper. The snout of the cannon was raised a few inches. When it roared again, the door was no more. The officer's sword fell; they charged. The doorway was stoutly defended but heavily outnumbered. The Roundheads forced their way in; those defenders that were cut off from the stairs were taken outside the castle and hacked and shot to death. The castle still resisted, as those on the spiral stairway were difficult to pass, and the battlements showered shot, boiling oil and rocks on the Roundheads below who were unable to get in. The officer shouted an order, and the Roundheads pulled back. From somewhere in the castle came a defiant cheer. It was short-lived. The cannons rose again, pieces flew from the battlements; it roared again and again until nothing *moved* on the battlements. A few Roundheads came out of the stable carrying straw. The officer's sword fell again. The Round-heads poured through the door again. The stairs still held. This time no attempt was made to take it. Straw was piled high and set alight. The stairs became a chimney, impossible to defend. Another order and the fire was doused with water, causing a last mighty puff of smoke. This time the Roundheads followed it up the stairs. The screaming started. It came on the breeze where we huddled. James' mind wandered from the horror. How good it must have been to own Poulakerry. A castle on a location of such beauty. The river Suir's silvery waters running through lush green pastures with the wooded mountains as green and purple background, and she there with him. The swans who had been scanning the water for food as they paddled gracefully downriver became startled; powerful wings lashed the air as they rose. James's eyes followed their flight; a child was flying over them, arms and legs jerking to gain purchase in the air. James' horrified mind thought he would land on a swan and so be saved. The swans were a hundred yards south of him. It was an illusion. Something small fell from the child's hands as he hit the ground, a bundle of broken flesh and bone. The pup. Through the broken battlements, James could see the screaming mother wrestling with two laughing soldiers. They tore the baby from her arms and flung it over the wall. She broke free they were having fun grabbing her and passing her one to the other, but she saw her chance and jumped to join her children. James looked at his men; they were waiting for orders.

'Tonight,' he said, 'we go back to Slievenamon.' James heard the word 'coward'; it was meant for his ears. He wanted to rise up and order them to attack, to kill and die in one futile gesture, but knew he could not; as in the middle of such slaughter, he would stand there guilt-ridden with each of their deaths, knowing there was no plan, no hope until put out of misery by some Roundhead glad of easy prey in the middle of the hate ridden orgy of death. James stood up and walked towards the one who had called 'coward'. He looked in his eyes as they closed. What he saw there caused him to stand aside. James walked through the trees; rabbits and squirrels scampered away, and birds fell silent as one of the only species capable of rising *above* them passed by, capable of rising above, but all too often falling far beneath.

CROMWELL

We watched as the horseman shouted for aid. Poulakerry was under attack. The mounted relief column quickly formed and left the town. We admired the plumed hats and shining steel as they passed our gate. There was little to admire in the few that returned. There was little time to dwell on their woes, as Cromwell's vanguard took up a position on the hill overlooking our gate. Four horsemen sat looking down at the town. A thousand musketeers filed past them. Then they waited. As a thousand cavalry trotted by, Wexford appeared at my elbow.

'I think they are trying to tell us something,' he observed. The parade was not over. Two thousand foot soldiers dressed in black, led by a bearded figure. 'Joshua,' Wexford put it in words. Joshua was staring down at the town; as he passed, even though he could not recognise me from that distance, I took a step back. Wexford gave me that mocking smile.

'Piss yourself?' he inquired. My retort was drowned out by a bugle, which announced the approach of the four horsemen. A white flag fluttered over their heads. Off to our right, the garrison leader watched as one rode closer to the wall and demanded the town open its gates and submit to the forces of the Parliament, and those within the walls of Clonmel would be under the protection of Oliver Cromwell. The garrison leader, in response, questioned the right of the lowly bred Cromwell to command a loyal subject of His Majesty to renege on his duty to the Crown.

'I will defend Clonmel to the death,' he concluded.

The horseman again. 'Am I to believe that the townspeople would also like to die for the Crown?' 'Sowing seeds of discontent,' observed Wexford. 'Present arms,' Wexford shouted. A line of muskets appeared along our battlements. The movement caught the eye of the horseman.

'The mercenaries, I believe,' he said. 'Men without cause or honour. Some fled Clonmel, their lives endangered by the town they came to protect. Yet ye remain. I will pay well for an open gate.'

'Shit, he is good,' Wexford said.

'Expect no help from Ormond,' the horseman continued. 'Where I am, he will not be. I know everything that happens in Clonmel town; you have no food for a long siege. What you will have in plenty is the plague. The sick turned away from Carrick you allowed entry. Think well on what I have said. Tomorrow the cannon speaks for me.

You have until then,' he wheeled his horse, rejoined the other three and was gone.

THE URCHIN

Wexford took Cromwell's message to heart. He gave instructions that the inner gate be closed. There would be no entry or exit without prior notice. The food was placed under guard and a ration system set up. Guards were posted on the only other way onto our street, the walk behind the battlements. At noon the following day, Wexford was on the walk looking up the hill at the cannon. He watched as the gunners packed the powder and ball. When the torch flared, he ordered his men off the wall. The cannon roared, and sods and grit sailed over the wall. The angry gunner's voice floated down on the breeze as he berated his team to raise the elevation. The next volley crashed into the wall; from where I was sheltering, I could see the wall shudder. Outside our street, I could hear the terrified screams of women and children. The next volley blew a hole in the battlements where Wexford and his men had vacated. Dust and splinters showered down upon them. The nearest garrison soldiers were not so lucky, blown off by granite and shredded steel.

The gunner was still not happy. The next round was on target; the outside gate burst into splinters, revealing the second gate under the arch, which the cannon could not reach. Then the gunner was silent. An officer shouted 'advance' and the Roundheads massed behind the cannon began their march on Clonmel. This time it was the turn of the Clonmel cannon directed by an officer on the wall. Gaps appeared in the advancing force, but they marched on. The cannon roared; destruction in its path again.

'Charge,' screamed the Roundhead, and they broke into a run, taking them inside the range of the cannon and safe from the impersonal killer.

Wexford was back on the wall. Muskets were discharged at the attackers, more loaded guns handed up. Still, they came. The garrison leader had waited for the last moment.

'Fire,' he ordered, and a line of attackers fell. Still, they came. A ladder was thrown against the broken battlements, and they began to swarm up it. Others could be heard under the arch battering at the gate. Soon the muskets were cast aside as hand to hand combat took place around the broken wall. Then a strange group of horsemen appeared, bending low in the saddle. Steel flashing, they cut into the Roundheads from the side. The attackers forced past our position, much to our relief.

The Roundhead cavalry charged down the hill and the muskets were reloaded, and they were used to pick off the cavalry as they passed. The attack was called off, leaving the strangers to introduce themselves. The promised reinforcements had arrived, led by Hugh Dubh O'Neill, through the west gate in triumph. A cheer rang along the battlements, fuelled by relief. I had the uneasy feeling that the attack was to test our strength and our weakness. I noted these things with a sense of detachment. The shadow of death had passed over me, and as I made my painful way around, I could see things in a different light. Wexford could see it, and he was puzzled. I no longer challenged his every action. He sometimes slapped me on the back, knowing it sent waves of pain through my shattered ribs. I knew it was because he wanted me back to my old annoying self. They let me through the gate every morning on my way to the river. There I sat for the day, eating my rations and watching the water flow. The children of the town gave me a wide berth as they bobbed for eels or fished for trout. Parliament troops patrolled the other side of the river. We would stare across at each other as they passed. Then the children returned to their fishing and me to gaze into the water. I had pulled a piece of bread from my ration bag and was chewing it slowly when I felt a presence. I dragged my eyes from the water and beheld an urchin. Age hard to guess, fifteen maybe, I thought, bony face and thin legs and arms sticking out of what I recognised as long ago had been grain sack. The sack was gathered at the waist by a length of string. We studied one another. He had old man's eyes. Things had been bad for him before things got bad.

'I have worms,' he informed me.

'Tell your mother,' I said. 'She will give you something.' He looked puzzled.

'I have no mother,' he said.

'Me neither,' I said glumly.

'But I have worms,' he sat beside me and produced a dog leaf tied with string. He opened the string; a mass of worms squirmed in its depth. 'I will give you the worms for a piece of bread. You could fish,' he prompted.

'Don't want worms. Don't want to fish,' I replied. I bit the bread and returned to watching the water flow by.

'Ah well,' he said popping a worm into his mouth and matching my slow chew. 'I would have preferred the bread.' I stopped chewing and looked at his bony side face as he slowly chewed the worm.

'If I wanted to fish, I could use the bread,' I pointed out.

'No good,' he replied. 'Too soft. Wash away in the water.' He swallowed and opened the dog leaf and carefully selected another worm; it was wriggling around his finger, heading for his mouth. Wordlessly, I handed him the bread. I noticed his chewing increased in speed as the bread disappeared. 'Cut a rod,' he said, nodding in the direction of an ash tree between swallows. I let Garcia's knife slip into my hand and I cut a six-foot length and handed it to him. He unwound the string from around his waist. At the end of the line was a length of hemp with a needle attached. One by one, he threaded the worms onto the hemp, then he tied a knot, making a wriggling ball of worms. He tied the string to the stick and handed it to me. I dropped the worms into the water. He went to walk away but changed his mind, and sat beside me looking into the water.

'What do I do now?' I asked.

'When you feel a bite on the worms, pull them out. The eel's teeth get caught on the hemp, and you swing him onto the bank.' We both returned to staring into the water. 'Won't happen do,' he said. 'Fished out. No one has caught any eels for days.' A trout rippled the water in the middle of the river.

'What about trout?' I asked.

'Maybe tonight,' he answered 'they come in closer to the bank.' We passed the day without fish. When it was time to go, I walked towards my gate. He followed. As I passed through the gate, he called me. 'Mister did you ever eat a worm?'

'No,' I said

'Don't bother, mister. They taste like shit.' He disappeared into the gloom.

'Did you have a good day, sir?' the sentry asked. He had asked the same question the previous day, and I had grunted and went on my painful way.

'Yes,' I said. 'I had a good day.' I started to laugh, but forgotten pain returned. Darkness fell, and I was back on the bank of the river watching the trout rise to the plentiful flies that floated down the river. The urchin appeared again and sat beside me. I lifted the worms and dipped them again in a different place.

'The trout won't take the worms until the flies are gone,' he advised me. There was a long silence. 'Not that it matters,' he said. The trout were not biting, but I was.

'Why,' I asked, 'does it not matter?'

'Hard to catch a trout with an eel bob,' he said and relapsed into silence. I sighed.

'What do I need?'

'Hooks,' he said. I reached into my rations and handed him the bread. He became a ball of action, eating food and putting worms on hooks that adorned his grain sack. The trout rise subsided. We waited expectantly. Then it happened; the line twitched. The excitement was too much for me. I jerked the rod upwards. Something silvery flashed past my nose and landed in the weeds of the bank. We were on our knees, searching when a voice behind me asked:

'What are you looking for?'

'Trout,' I replied, my eyes were searching the gloom.

'You should try the river,' he suggested. I could see him now, or part of him – his face. He was dressed all in black, sitting in a black boat. Something silvery gave a last hop and splashed into the water; my catch had escaped.

'Who are you?' I challenged.

'Who are you?' he countered. I hesitated

'Landers,' I said.

'Good,' he said. 'I can stay in the boat. Power they call me, poacher Power. Your brother wants you to be here every night, this time for information and supplies. He said to be sure no one outside our street knows. Trout,' he said, landing a basket full on the bank and silently glided away.

'Now,' I said to the urchin. 'I have a basket of trout and a boy who knows too much.' We thought about it for a while. He put it in words

'It's time to go home.' We walked to our street. To my dismay, Wexford was talking to the sentry. They stopped talking as we approached.

'What have you got there, Lazuras?' He had taken to calling me Lazuras in an attempt to annoy me.

'Trout,' I said.

'No, the thing carrying them,' Wexford caught the grain sack and lifted its contents into the air in front of my nose. 'No outsiders in our street,' he reminded me.

I explained. 'He knows about our supplies and information arriving by river each night, and how long would that last if news got out to hungry townspeople and Cromwell's spies?' Wexford pulled the grain sack closer so that the urchin's nose was touching his.

'We could cut his throat. Who would miss him?'

'I would,' I said.

'Why?' he asked, easing his grip on the bag.

'I have a poe under the bed that needs attention every day, as has every other house.' They stood aside and let us pass. We went to my house which I shared with others, but I had my room due to my wounds. The kitchen, with an open fireplace, we passed through. My bed against the wall had two blankets. I took one and threw it on the floor. 'Yours,' I said. We went back into the kitchen. The fire was dying; we fed it with wood. We got the iron skillet and hung it on the crane, swung it over the flame. We ate trout until we could eat no more. The smell blew down the street; soon, heads popped in the door. We cooked the fish and threw it on the table to be devoured by those strong enough to hold their place. The day had taken its toll on me. I retired to my room, pulled the poe out and deposited a sizeable fishy turd into it, and left it out so that my new housemate could see it in the morning. I drifted off into a sound sleep. When I woke in the morning, he was already up. 'Well? I asked. 'What have you to say?' He looked at me with those old man eyes.

'Thanks,' he said, 'for not letting them cut my throat.'

'Thanks for the trout.' I put my foot against the poe and pushed it towards him; he caught it up and looked into it.

'And thanks for the job,' he finished. He left on his first of many trips to the river.

THE TOWN

The cannon roared every day at the same time. Then they seemed content to camp and wait. They were content to keep us sealed in while they tightened their hold on the town. A night-time visit by the poacher brought the news that river patrols made it too dangerous for him to bring supplies, but a large shipment was already waiting in the woods across the river. We would need to cross the river to engage the patrols from Carrick and Cahir while the supplies were brought across. The fear was that when Cromwell returned, there might not be another delivery. I climbed the ladder to the battlements. I heard the patter of bare feet, behind me. The boy was looking up at me.

'Come on,' I said. The battlements at each side of our street were controlled by the garrison. The commander was not to be seen as we descended into the town. We walked past the town hall. The townspeople watched us pass; some crossed themselves. 'What is the matter with them?' I muttered to myself.

'You have not been to Mass then?' the boy said; his ears were good. I took a closer look. It was like his ears had grown to the size he should be.

'Why?' I asked.

'Ye are ex, ex,' he stuttered.

'Excommunicated,' I finished for him.

'Yes, that too,' he agreed. The smell hit me first as we entered Irishtown. I looked at the boy. 'My old home,' he said. The street ran with human and animal waste. Some buildings had black crosses on the doors. I turned to the boy. 'Plague,' he said. We came to a church. There was a building alongside. He took my hand and led me towards it. The door was open. A line of small beds both sides. The users of the beds sat at a long table. They were looking at a door further in where steam was bringing the smell of cooking. A woman came through the door. The mayor's wife. She was carrying a large pot, while another with a spoon slopped gruel on the plates in front of my urchin's lookalikes. The love of my life was using the spoon. They were at the end of the table before they noticed us.

'Late breakfast,' I observed, because I was flustered. The mayor's wife looked at me in the way I had become accustomed to, like I had somehow let her down.

'Breakfast, dinner and supper,' she snapped. I noticed behind her, breakfast, dinner and supper was already gone. I tried to catch the eye of my beloved; she was looking behind me.

'Hello, Tom,' she said. 'Where have you been?' My heart sank. She had forgotten my name. 'Hello, Miss. I was with my friend,' the urchin replied. From deep within me came a sense of shame. I had made him eat worms when he was starving and gave him a job carrying shit, and he called me a friend.

'Are you coming back to us, Tom?' she asked.

'No, I am going to be a soldier just like him,' he said, looking up at me. 'I am staying with him, even if the priest says I will be ex-something.' The mayor's wife broke into the conversation.

'How is your side? she asked.

'Better,' I said.

'Well, look after it. I don't want to have to wrap you up again. I will be too busy cooking dinner.' I was dismissed. As I walked away, I heard her say, 'Thank the garrison leader for the food. I am sure it was not given lightly.' I could feel Tom's eyes on me as we walked to the west gate. O'Neill's men were billeted around it. They were grazing their horses while a line of sentries kept a lookout. I asked to see O'Neill.

'Landers to see you,' I heard announced. O'Neill looked like a man who wished he was somewhere else. I reached out my hand. He ignored it.

'What do you want?' he asked.

'The river patrol from Cahir. You need to keep them at bay. We will engage the patrol from Carrick; this will give us time to bring food across.'

'Why risk my men on the other side of the river? Ormond will bring supplies. We will wait for them.'

'Cromwell has gone to ensure nothing gets here,' I pointed out. 'Meanwhile, they sit up there using cannon, hunger and disease to keep us busy until he comes back.'

'I am planning an attack on the cannon,' O'Neill said. 'Would you help me with that?' he challenged.

'No,' I said. 'I am informed that there are a thousand muskets in the wilderness waiting and hoping for just that. I was also requested to thank you for coming to our aid during the assault, and to advise you against doing it again, as they will be expecting it.' He looked at me like I had two heads.

'Go back to your den of thieves,' he said. 'I will send no men across the river and trust you to get them back.'

As we walked back through the town, I noticed all food shops shut, but the barber and the draper side by side were open. I looked in the window of the barbershop – a bearded and rough-looking tramp stared out at me. My reflection. And then there was that smell I smelled under my arm. It was bad, but it was not me. My gaze fell on Tom. I sniffed, and my nose recoiled in horror. 'Come,' I said. The barber was talking to a very pretty girl who was sweeping hair off the floor. She flashed me a smile as I sat in the chair. The barber jerked his head, and the girl went into the back room. 'Daughter?' I asked, trying to make conversation. He studied me for a moment. I was looking at myself in the mirror, trying to remember what I used to look like.

'Wife,' he said.

'I need a shave, haircut and a bath,' I said.

'You certainly do,' he agreed. He lathered my face and began to edge the razor. He leaned over me and began to shave my throat. I shut up then. I was nervous about the sharp blade near my neck. He stopped to wipe the blade. I continued.

'Would your wife do the bath for me? You know how hard it is to get to some places.' He was coming at me again. I was glad he had finished my throat as his hand was shaking. He must have missed a spot. He raised my chin. 'That boy needs a good wash,' I said. He called his wife to wash Tom and began to shave again.

'You are one of them,' he accused. 'Brave defenders of a town that the ordinary people in it just want to live in peace. I have a young wife. I want children. We went to the mayor. We begged him to take terms. The priests were there; the bishop had decreed the town should stand up and fight for our faith, fight for our God. The garrison commander, a man who thinks the King is God. The mercenaries who ran people out of their homes, coin is their God. We, the townspeople, will be sacrificed on the altar of their Gods. Think of that when you count your coins, if indeed you survive this hateful mess.' Chastened, I said, 'I am going next door to the drapers.' The rant had calmed him.

'I would leave your purse here if I were you.' He went back to cutting hair.

A small, smartly dressed man measured me with his eyes as I walked through the door.

'Boy,' I explained, 'about that tall.' I held my hand to my chest. He placed garments on the counter. I nodded.

'With clothes like that, he will need matching socks,' the draper gushed.

'He does not need socks,' I said. 'He goes barefoot.'

'How right you are, sir,' he said. 'Socks are no use without shoes. Those should suit his height with room to grow into.' Shoes were grabbed from under the counter and placed with the socks. I pulled out my purse. He shook his head sadly. 'Surely you do not mean to walk beside a boy I have dressed in such,' he looked me up and down, 'rags?' he concluded.

'The bandages,' I started.

'Yes, I understand sir. They are soiled. You need a jacket to cover them up.' He produced a tunic, black with gold braid. He quickly wrapped around me and buttoned it up.

'And breeches, sir.' With the air of a magician, a red one appeared from under the counter. 'You can try them on over there, sir.' I got behind a curtain and forced them on.

'Too tight,' I said.

'Certainly not, sir. That is all the fashion now. May I compliment you on how you fill them. You are quite the model, sir. They are worn with knee-length leather boots. These, sir, will complete the picture.' Boots smelling of leather and polish were produced. I put them on. I liked them. He stood back to admire me. 'You, sir, are quite the gent; perfect, but for lack of a hat. May I be so bold?' he did not wait for an answer, taking a plumed hat from the shelf behind him and placing it on my head at a jaunty angle. He stood back to view me better and concluded. 'I am in awe, sir. You look truly magnificent.'

'How much?' I asked. He told me how much. I asked again with disbelief. Bemused, I paid him. 'And those, sir?'

he indicated my old clothes that he was holding at arm's length.

'How do you keep going? I asked.

'What else can I do?' he stood in the doorway still holding my old rags.

'Sell them to Cromwell,' I suggested. I smiled at him, and he smiled back. I went back to the barbershop. The barber was still working.

'Told you so,' he said without looking up. I walked to the back room. It had gone quiet. I opened the door and threw the clothes on the floor. The girl had him in a towel, drying him. Startled, he swung around. I noticed why he had gone quiet. Life goes on, I thought. Life goes on.

PIMP

Tom had begun to leave for long periods. He was passing by when I caught him by the expensive collar.

'What are you up to?' I asked him suspiciously.

'Helping with my old home, sir,' he answered. 'You remember, breakfast, dinner and supper.'

'You are helping the mayor's wife,' and my voice trailed off.

'Yes,' he said. I released my grip. He straightened his jacket, and walked down our street. Everyone he passed seemed to have a word for him. Then again, he knew them all, and I who had fought with them and drank with them did not, but then I never emptied their poes, I thought. He would stop to speak now and then; sometimes he pointed in my direction; where he got his clothes, I thought. Then I caught some strange comments about my red pants and the tunic with the gold braid.

'Funny how they all look the same, yes they all look different,' another said. I thought about it and how men seemed to avoid me. I look like an officer, I thought. They resent that. Wexford was the worst. He gave me a mock salute every time he met me, telling me once when I challenged him, 'You look the part,   officer.' I thought they were jealous now that I looked like one. It was alright when I looked like a tramp, like them. I would show them. After the usual midday cannon fire, I would strut down our street swinging a blackthorn stick in the air. The stick had a function, as the itch under the bandages could only be reached by stick, but not in front of the envious observers. The cannon had stopped, but the church bells did not. They reminded me of a time long ago when I blessed myself for the Angelus, and they told me it was time for Mass or, like now, that another burial was taking place. They had scarcely stopped when they started again. The priests were busy, I thought, but not so busy that two were being prevented from entry by the sentry at the end of our street, Tom between them by an ear and arm. They were talking to the sentry who turned and pointed at me. I was walking towards them when Wexford passed me, his face livid; he was making straight for the priests. The sentry stood between them.

'The bells,' Wexford shouted. 'The bells, stop them damn bells.' I arrived at the scene and stood between Wexford and the priests.

'The bells are annoying,' I said, 'but there is no need for violence.'

'Is that him?' one priest asked the sentry, pointing at me. The sentry nodded.

'No need for violence?' stormed Wexford. 'One burial after another. Why don't I throw ye outside the walls to tell them in person. The people are dying like flies.'

'Ye could bury them in the morning at the same time as a Mass bell and at six the Angelus bell,' I said. The priest agreed, as they did not think about the message they were sending out. 'There,' I said, 'no need for roaring and shouting,' pleased I had shown leadership qualities in front of the upstart Wexford.

'Do you own this boy?' the priest asked. Tom was trying to catch my eye; a difficult task, as his ears were being twisted in two different directions.

'I do,' I said.

'So you are the whoremaster,' they roared. Wexford turned towards me, looked me up and down. 'Do you have to ask?'

'What?' I roared. I raised my blackthorn stick and was about to bring it down. Wexford caught my arm.

'No need for roaring and shouting and violence,' he smirked. 'Let them speak.' One priest cleared his throat and began to introduce himself. 'Get on with,it' said Wexford. It became clear through confession that sex was available through a boy operating from the godless mercenary's street. The boy belonged to one of the leaders, and all proceeds went to him. He also said his master would slit the throat of anyone who would hurt him.

'Is that right boy?' the priest said, giving Tom an extra twist on his ear.

'He said that, did he?' I asked, my temper dying down, fixing the nearest priest with a malevolent stare. He did not understand, until he saw the dagger which I had let slip into my hand. They let Tom go. He ran behind me. They were not finished. They addressed Wexford.

'What are you going to do about it?' I was getting mad again. Wexford said, 'Nothing, I have known about it for weeks, good for the men.' He turned, gave me that smirk and left.

'He did not know,' Tom blurted to the priests. 'He did not know.'

'Is that true?' the priest asked.

'I am responsible for the boy and things done in my name,' I said tiredly. 'There are men here who have heard not the word of God or his forgiveness for a long time. That, you are responsible for.' 'Fr Casey fears for his life, and you excommunicated,' the priest pointed out.

'But not them,' I indicated the street. 'Fr Casey could come here, say Mass here, and hear confessions under my protection.' It was arranged.

'Now, Tom,' I said, 'back to the house.' We walked in the door. 'Now, Tom,' I said. 'It's time for this.' I raised the blackthorn stick. His eyes looked into mine. I remembered a dog I had once, who had chased a sheep I did not want chased, who came back to me for praise but instead got a smack. I lowered the stick.

'What am I going to do with you?' I asked aloud.

'You could bring me back to my old home,' he said, and the more I thought about, the more it seemed right. Back through the Irish quarters we went. The stench was worse.

Bodies lay in blankets in front of the church. Waiting for the Angelus, I thought. We went into Tom's orphanage. The place was clean and tidy. Children played on the floor. They looked bright-eyed and healthy. The mayor's wife came out of the kitchen. When she saw me her face lit up. She came for me, arms outstretched, and hugged me.

'I knew you would be kind,' she said. I could see over her shoulder. Tom was smiling. A strange woman came out of the kitchen. 'She is not allowed to come here anymore,' the mayor's wife said, 'since you took over.' The pieces began to form in my mind. Tom's happy face a further clue. She left then to help in the kitchen. Tom said, 'I could see the way they treated you your last visit. I am sorry your woman left.' Not much past him, I thought. Then another thought struck me.

'Who were the women you used?'

'Down the end,' he said. I looked. Two teenage girls were smiling up at me. I could see the need for confession for their customers.

'Young,' I said shocked.

'They were old when they were twelve,' Tom replied, but the happiness had left his eyes. He shrugged. 'But that is over now.' He thought for a while, then said, 'Sorry'.

'Sorry for what?' I asked.

'I did it in your name; it's your problem now.'

'I was on the wall when they came riding hard, fifty or sixty men looking for the garrison leader, around the wall, next gate, fast,' added Wexford, watching the cannon crew on the hill. 'I found out the next morning that they were a section of Ormond's proposed relief. There would be no relief, no supplies. I also found out they were billeted in the house near the church, where the mayor's wife had fed the orphans. I found this out when the mayor's wife came to the gate complete with orphans, looking for me.' Wexford had a tantrum, saying, 'No, no, no. Only soldiers in here.' 'Soldiers? You want soldiers? You will get soldiers?'

'No, no,' he started. I pulled a boy out of the bunch. 'Look at him. He looks like your son,' I interrupted. He gave me a long look.

'Keep them away from me, and they are going to cause trouble,he said' pointing to the girls.

'He had given up, Tom,' I said. 'Your army. I passed the power down like an officer would and made to scuttle away.'

'My army need muskets,' Tom said.

'Your army? Your army?' I repeated. 'Most of your army could not lift a musket.'

'Just one,' he bargained.

'Alright,' I said.

'For a start,' he added. I produced a musket.

'Powder and ball,' he demanded.

'Ball,' I said. 'No powder.' We glared at each other. 'No powder,' I repeated. I went to the storeroom and selected a musket from a box that had come with the supplies. We had not used them as we could not find where the match was placed and looked different from the muskets we were using. I cocked it and pulled the trigger. A spark flickered. I did it again; again it sparked. I picked up a small bag of grain. Tom had brought a table out into the street. I planked the musket down on the table. 'Musket,' I said.

'Ball' I planked a bag of balls on the table. 'The grain powder,' I said. He looked at me.

'Powder?' he questioned. I poured the grain into the musket, dropped the ball in, put in the wadding, packed it with the ram, pulled the trigger. The spark flew.

'Bang,' I said. The urchins gathered around Tom. I left them to it. Days passed. I asked Tom how his army was getting on.

'We need real powder,' he said.

'What's wrong with the grain?' I asked.

'They keep eating it,' Tom admitted.

I said, 'If I had given you real powder, you would not want to be around the fire when they fart.' I went away chuckling at the humour of it, but I could see Tom was not amused.

'I need real powder,' he called after me. The poacher came with the news. A large consignment of food was on its way from Dungarvan. They would wait in the woods for a waving torch. They would then drop their cargo on the riverbank and run. I began to address the problem of getting the supplies across the river in the dark. The bridge across the river was guarded by an encampment of troops, reinforced by patrols from Carrick and Cahir. The barges we had brought with us the first day were available. They were large, unwieldy crafts usually pulled by horse upriver or floated down. I had an idea of using one as a ferry. This idea involved getting a coil of rope across quietly onto an oak tree upstream of our street, my enjoyment of fishing blighted by the problem of how to get this done. And if done, would it work? Staring into the deep dark swirling water did not help. I stared at the length of rope.

'I need to get that on a tree,' I explained. Tom looked at me, troubled.

'Is it because of me,' he asked, or the woman?' I was not listening to him. I could hear the hoofbeats on the other side recede towards Carrick.

'How long would it take?' I mused aloud.

'Depends on the drop,' Tom said, lost in some nightmare of his own. 'Took my da five minutes. He stole a lamb. It tasted nice, though. I don't want to be left alone again.' I looked from the rope to Tom; my mouth dropped open.

'Tom,' I said. 'I need to tie that rope to that tree on the other side, then to the barge; the current will swing it out, a pole will push it to the other side, then a rope from here can pull it back. We can ferry men over and supplies back.'

'Why did you not say that?' Tom asked.

'I thought I did,' I replied. Tom took the end of the rope and slid into the river. I paid out the rope as he faded into the dark. Then the rope went slack. I began to pace the bank.

'Worried were you?' It was Tom. The current had carried him downstream. The drag was too great. He admitted, 'I had to let go of the rope.' I hurried the shivering Tom back to our house. He began to dress, frozen fingers fumbling with buttons.

'Your old clothes were better,' I pointed out. 'Pull it over your head and tie it with string.'

'Pity string would not draw a barge,' Tom observed. 'I could pull string across.'

'The string could pull a rope,' I said excitedly. I went to Wexford to explain my plan. He looked doubtful, but knew as I did that without the food we were doomed. When the patrol past Tom slid into the water, I unrolled the twine. After what seemed too long, I felt three tugs on the string.

'He got there,' Wexford said, surprised. The rope was next. The thought struck me, would the tug be too much, even on land? Then came the three tugs again. We tied the rope to the barge. Wexford beckoned, and his men climbed silently aboard. We handed them a line and a pole. Wexford and I crossed with the next group. Then we split, Wexford and one group taking the Carrick side, and I led my group past the old oak that held our ferry. The team left on the barge, lit a torch and waved it. They came out of the trees, carts loaded with everything we might need.

The barge was loaded and pulled home, unloaded and pulled back. The barge was filled again. I heard the rattle of chains as the carts drove back to the trees, empty. Then the thunder of hoofs as the patrol returned from Carrick, followed by the musket fire from Wexford and his men. The flashes lit up the river, and we could see the barge going back with its last load. Then the patrol from the Cahir side came at the gallop. I shouted 'fire', and the first row of horses and men went down. The rest quickly dismounted and returned fire. In the total darkness, all could be seen was the flash of the muskets. The sound of battle from the Carrick side died down. My brain was confronted with a flaw in my plan. Wexford had withdrawn and was going home with the barge. The Carrick soldiers faced with no resistance would push forwards. The barge could not come back for us; we were trapped between both patrols. Back to the tree came a whisper in my ear. The grass shook as Tom the whisperer went from man to man. We began to withdraw. The rope from the tree became our escape route as we waded into the river. Musket fire erupted behind us. In the dark, the Carrick and Cahir patrols were shooting at each other. As we neared the bank, I could see Wexford peering at the opposite bank.

'I did not want you getting wet,' I said, teeth chattering as we emerged from the water. We had lost two men, but our store was full. The firing had awoken the town. They had seen the laden barges and knew we had food, and the town was starving.

LOAVES AND FISHS

They came in their hundreds; women, children, beggars and cripples. We closed the gate, glad of James' foresight in erecting it. We doubled the guard on the battlements. Wexford and I went to the gates in an attempt to restore order. They were gone past reason. They pressed against the entrance, waved hands through the bars. Some tried to shove small children through. Still, they came. The ones at the gate now squashed against it. Some of them began to faint. Then shots rang out. The cries of hunger turned to panic. They began to run, leaving their dead behind them, clearing the way for us to see a line of soldiers on the other bank firing into the crowd.

Behind them other soldiers making camp. There would be no more trips across the river. No more fishing. No more peaceful walks. The siege of Clonmel was tightening. Tom pulled at my tunic. 'Now can we have powder?'

'Yes, Tom,' I agreed.

'And two more muskets?' he added. I was thinking about the riverbank ground lost. I thought. 'Yes, Tom.' I handed him the powder and two muskets. He stuck his head out the door and whistled. His army came out of nowhere.

'Table and chairs,' he ordered. 'You carry the muskets,' Tom asked. I followed them; The men laughed as we passed. Some of them propositioned the girls, something I would have to confront. I saw the need for the table, as a shot hit it as we walked behind it. 'Here will do,' said Tom. They set down the table on its edge. 'Chair,' Tom sat with some ceremony on the chair. 'Muskets,' he requested. I slid him the weapons from my lying position behind the table. The urchins knelt in a circle behind the table.

'Powder boy,' Tom called. The powder boy, who was a girl, took a musket and measured in the powder.

'Ball,' she called. A small boy popped in the ball.

The next boy used the ram to pack it down and handed it to Tom. While this was happening, the second musket was moving around the line. I was impressed. Then Tom fired. The chair blew over backwards, and Tom became entangled with the boy with the shot. The musket flew through the air. I caught it before it collided with my head. Tom got to his feet as if nothing had happened. 'Musket,' he called. He was handed the second musket. 'Chair,' he called; the second girl braced herself against the chair. Tom fired again, rewarded by a yelp from the other bank. Tom handed the empty back and received a loaded replacement. I peered over the table; they had been standing taking shots at us. Tom fired; one of them went down. They began to back away as Tom fired again and another limped away. 'Some things you can't learn using grain,' he chided as he fired again. 'Now they know this is still our bank.' The haggling started the next day. The priests came first, slipping fearfully through our gate under the protection of Tom and his group. I gave them our house for confessions. Then they said Mass in the street. I could see it meant a lot to our troops.

Tom was standing next to me, watching. I blessed myself and knelt. Tom did the same. The sermon was about loaves and fishes, and how God saw the need to feed the multitude. Wexford came and looked down on me.

'Rise. I forgive you,' he smirked. I jumped to my feet. 'They,' he indicated the priests, 'want to meet us after Mass. I wonder why?' he finished sarcastically. I felt sorry for the priests. They asked the Mass-goers for food donations, as coin was no longer of use. They came in the door of Wexford's house. Wexford sat behind the table, and I sat on it. The older one spoke.

'The town needs food.'

'The town who would have us killed need food,' Wexford sneered. 'O'Neill, who refused to help us get it, needs food. Two men died to get food for their comrades. You will find no loaves and fishes here.'

'I second that,' I said, 'however the labourer is worthy of his hire. I require a wedding service and a Mass for our fallen friends. We will pay in food for the needy.' I went out. Our soldiers were eying up two of Tom's soldiers. Remembering the auction at Landers' Hall, I stood up on a table pulling one of Tom's girls with me. 'Who wants this girl?' I shouted. I heard one say, 'Good. He is back in business.'

'Bids will be taken in rations and are not refundable. They will be given to the poor. Now where are all those great men from yesterday who boasted of their manhood as this girl went to war?'

'We are just after confession and Mass,' protested one.

'All taken care of. The priest has assured me no sin will stain the soul of anyone who contributes to this worthy cause. Tom,' I called my assistant. 'Can you write?

'The mayor's wife taught me,' Tom said proudly.

'Take down the bids. Come on men,' I said.

'All today's rations,' said one. 'It's for a good cause.'

'One day's ration from a hypocrite on my left,' I called to Tom. There was general laughter. A sense of fun soon took over. I gave her a twirl, which caused another spate of bids. I brought up the second girl, proclaiming she was an excellent cook, not that it will matters for days.

'No,' I said. 'Not what you are thinking. To procure this lady will mean you will have nothing left to cook.' More ribald laughter. She sold well. 'Now, gentlemen. The auction over, it only remains for the girls to make their choice of man.' One girl jumped off the table and grabbed a man. The other hesitated; she was looking at me.

'You are the only one,' she whispered. She paused as her face reddened.

'I did not bid,' I whispered desperately.

'You are the only one I never had,' she finished.

'Pick the best of them,' I said relieved. She jumped off the table and linked her man.

'Fr Casey will now conduct the weddings,' I said loudly. Fr Casey, hearing his name, popped out and whatever out-cry was about to erupt was swallowed. Fr Casey had a brief meeting with the couples and decided to go ahead with the wedding. Everyone in Irishtown would have a meal and I had passed on the problem of the girls.

THE GUNNER

The cannon on the hill fell silent. Strangely, this was worrying. We lounged around on the wall looking up the slope. Then we saw them, the four horsemen. Cromwell was back. The four horsemen hoisted the white flag and walked their horses downhill.

'Here we go again,' said Wexford. The horseman rode within earshot and called out, 'I salute you. You are brave men. Why must you die? The king will be executed, the priests who have stirred up this trouble will be executed, O'Neill's dream of returning to his former glory is just that – a dream. Why must you die for a dream that was over long before Lord Cromwell set foot on this land? Those of you who fight for coin, leave this place. You will not be harmed.'

'Who offers this safe passage?' Wexford shouted. The portly sergeant looked at the man beside him, who nodded.

'Lord Cromwell,' the sergeant replied.

'Just wanted to be sure,' Wexford raised the musket, but the horsemen had galloped off. Cromwell looked down on the town. Clonmel would fall like all the others, of that he was sure. There would be more glowing letters of praise, like the ones received for Drogheda and Wexford. He knew what they meant. The dead had no use for houses or land, but the army would need them. Ships were carrying slaves out in increasing numbers; wrong religion, wrong loyalty, wrong place, equal reasons for deportation. He shuddered. Somewhere in the back of his mind, he was afraid; of what, he did not know. God? Joshua? Royalists and their sense of entitlement? He cast his thoughts back to Clonmel. Hunger, plague, surrender or Joshua – he shuddered again. He wondered if he was coming down with something. He prayed for health so he could continue God's work.   The garrison leader, fuelled by suspicion, we might take the offer of free passage, came to the battlements to offer reinforcements, saying we were in the line of the main attack and only the inside gate stood between the enemy and us. Wexford declined his offer. He then raised the matter of food shortage. I called Wexford and had a whispered conversation.

'A cart of supplies for a cannon?' Wexford offered.

'Why a cannon?' the leader asked.

'If they hack down the gate, they will face the cannon,' Wexford explained. It was agreed. When darkness fell, we made the swap. I could not wait for morning. It was a novelty for me. I enlisted two of Garcia's men to be on my team. I, of course, would be the chief gunner. I admired the sleek iron barrel, the pile of balls that were stacked beside it, and the barrel of powder.

'Load,' I ordered my crew. I watched as they loaded. It was like the muskets, powder and ball, except for more powder and bigger ball. The shaft by which it was towed was left on the ground to stabilise it, and there were chocks behind the wheels. The barrel was raised, lowered by a winch system and held in the required position with an iron pin. Wexford and one of his cronies came to inspect the gun. I glowered at him. 'I command the cannon,' I told him firmly.

Wexford nudged his friend.

'Such a man,' he said. 'He comes back from the dead, raises an urchin army, brings religion back into the street. Now commands the cannon. Should I fear for my position?' Wexford asked his companion. I looked at Wexford suspiciously. His face was serious. They walked away and were climbing onto the battlements before they burst into laughter.

'Give it its highest elevation,' I told my gunners. 'The torch,' I requested. I brought the flame to touch the hemp. 'Mark,' I shouted. Wexford broke off his conversation and looked down. 'Mark,' I cried again. The cannon roared. Wexford hit the ground, his friend on top of him. The ball whooshed over his head. Wexford was on his feet, swearing at me. 'Can you see where it hit?' I asked calmly. He looked out over the parapet.

'Yes,' he said.

'Good,' I said. 'Now mark the next.' The cannon was lowered.

'Wait,' Wexford called as he moved away from the path of the shot.

'That will teach him not mock us,' I said. It was our turn to laugh. We fired two more before we lost elevation to clear the wall. We were ready for the next attack.

LORD STAPLETON

Lord Stapleton had approached Cromwell, not as a powerful ally but a defeated liability looking for help. The humiliation would stay with him forever. Cromwell had refused to help, citing the need to keep his force strong and united, rather than dispatching his men to settle petty disputes. He had joined the army little better ranked than the sons of wealthy merchants whose father had bought them a place. He had distinguished himself in battle with his newly acquired knowledge of the mindset of the ordinary people. After Wexford, he had been given his command, as Cromwell turned for Dublin for the winter. With the promise of rich pickings and a cosy winter, his command followed as he turned for home and Landers' Hall. Lord Woodford had received word that Cromwell had retired for the winter, was so unprepared for an attack that the first he knew about it was a sword held to his throat in his bed. His officers murdered in their sleep, and Lord Stapleton had given the soldiers a choice of death or joining him on his assault on Landers' Hall.

Lord Woodford was placed on his horse and brought along. There was no need to attack Landers' Hall. The gates were opened when he announced himself. To his surprise, everything was as he left it. Faith, Hope and Charity hurried to meet him, bowing and scraping the same as usual.

'You have kept the place well,' he praised. 'I trust the corn is in the barn where I left it?'

'Yes, your Lordship,' Hope stuttered.

'Every grain,' Faith assured him.

'He would not let us take any,' Charity added.

'He?' questioned the lord. Could it be? he thought. 'Landers?' he guessed out loud.

'No, your Lordship. His Lordship.'

Lord Stapleton turned to his sergeant.

'Bring him up here.' Lord Woodford, still in his nightgown, was brought forward. 'Hang him up there.' Stapleton indicated the torch holder over the gate. 'Small thanks I admit for saving my corn.'

'What? What?' Woodford looked bewildered as he was hauled up by the neck. Stapleton watched Woodford as he danced on air; there was something undignified about being hung in a nightgown. He thought of the shame he had endured in the hall. Did hanging Woodford help? No, he knew it would always be with him until he caught up with Landers. Landers. How he hated that name. He turned to Faith, Hope and Charity.

'Let it be known that I will flog anyone who calls my abode 'Landers' Hall'.'

'Yes, sir,' Faith agreed.

'We wouldn't,' Hope said.

'We don't call it that anymore, sir,' Charity added. They began shoving each other.

'Go,' Stapleton hissed. They ran. 'Now,' Lord Stapleton said. 'I trust my kitchen is as well preserved as my barn.' He turned towards the great house; it was good to be home, he thought, pushing in the front door. A nun confronted him.

'Welcome to the bishop's palace,' she said. 'His Lordship Bishop Watkins has yet to rise. Whom shall I say is waiting?'

KILKENNY

Lord Stapleton looked out over his domain from the window where he had hung two priests. Spring had brought new life to his estate. Ned was ploughing. Birds sang. Faith, Hope and Charity had come and gone, taking with them the good news that despite the war, rents would remain unchanged. Below him, his men were saddling up. A courier had arrived bringing orders to proceed with all haste to Kilkenny. He sighted; it did not seem that important anymore. He wondered was it because Landers was dead. He looked back at the table at the man who had signed the death warrant.

'Finish your breakfast, bishop. We are moving out.'

Kilkenny. The cavalcade of dead and wounded passed them as they approached the command post. Cromwell's right-hand man came striding towards him. Lord Stapleton surveyed the fat officer with distaste. The feeling was mutual.

'Why have you not been here to assist in the attack?' the portly one demanded.

'I left it in your capable hands,' Lord Stapleton replied before adding, 'Not doing so well, are we? Take me to your master, my good man.' The sergeant swallowed his reply and led the way to the command tent. Cromwell was not happy. Kilkenny had two defensive lines – Irishtown, held by the townspeople, and inside that a heavily fortified walled town with professional soldiers. Cromwell pointed out, 'We have suffered heavy losses and are no nearer to success. We may have to lift the siege.'

'Have you offered them terms?' Lord Stapleton asked.

'If you were here, you would know?' The portly sergeant sneered.

'I am here now,' Lord Stapleton said. 'I would like to approach Irishtown with the same terms.' 'Do you think you will do better than me?' the fat man was getting angry.

'Could I possibly do worse?' Lordy answered.

'Enough,' Cromwell said sharply. 'If Lord Stapleton wants to give terms, let him do so.'

'I will call them for you,' the sergeant offered.

'That will not be necessary,' Lord Stapleton said. 'But perhaps you could use that magnificent,' he paused, looking at the sergeant's girth, 'voice to call a ceasefire. I would not like to be shot during my endeavours.' Lord Stapleton returned to his men. 'White flag and the bishop,' he requested. He went to his supply wagon. A bag containing the ceremonial robes were handed to the bishop. Together they rode towards Irishtown. A word to his men saw them clustered around him as he passed by the black-clad Joshua and his men. They saw the regally clad Bishop Watkins and lost all reason. They charged the horses, using bare hands to drag riders to the ground to get to the bishop.

'Keep them back,' Lord Stapleton shouted as he grabbed the bridle of the bishop's horse and, white flag fluttering, galloped towards Irishtown. 'Hold a line of muskets levelled at them from the walls. I seek entry,' Lord Stapleton called.

'Who are you and what is your business here?' a leader had emerged.

'I am Lord Stapleton, and this is your bishop who has been my guest for the winter. I have persecuted the Church in the past and wish to repent, in some small fashion. I am returning your bishop unharmed and well treated. As you may have seen, I can no longer guarantee his safety. It is his wish to die with you, his flock, as it is your wish to die for your king. I will ask the cannon be silent today that you may welcome your bishop and make your peace with God.' The gate opened, and Bishop Watkins rode into Kilkenny. Lord Stapleton had fired his greatest weapon straight into the heart of Irishtown.

THE FALL OF KILKENNY

The next morning, Lord Stapleton sat in Cromwell's command tent, as the portly one paced the tent impatiently.

'Why?' he asked. 'Why are the cannon silent?'

'Lord Stapleton has requested that, given time, he can reduce the defences without the use of cannon,' Cromwell answered.

'They are using the ceasefire to rebuild their defences,' the sergeant protested. 'I wish to resume the bombardment.'

'I find the silence relaxing,' Lord Stapleton said, 'and I would ask you to contribute to that silence.' The sergeant stopped pacing.

'What did you say?' he demanded.

'I invited you to participate in the beauty of silent meditation,' Lord Stapleton replied.

'You can resume cannon fire in an hour,' Cromwell settled the disagreement with authority. The sergeant looked at his watch and lapsed into the requested silence.

'Rider coming, sir,' the voice from a soldier outside the tent broke the moody impasse.

The commander of Irishtown, under a white flag, sat his horse outside the tent. The sergeant bolted out to grab the horse.

'What is it you want?' he demanded.

'I would speak to Lord Stapleton.'

'What is it you want?' This time the voice more threatening than before.

'My apologies for the sergeant,' Lord Stapleton said from the tent. 'The roar of the cannon has made him quite deaf.' The rider continued.

'It is the decision of the people of Irishtown to take terms, and we will leave if given safe passage, escorted through your lines by Lord Stapleton.' Cromwell had come from his tent. 'I will write that on this day, the command of Irishtown, having offered fierce resistance, have on this day taken terms, and at noon will be escorted safely through our lines by Lord Stapleton.' The horseman turned and rode back to Irishtown. Lord Stapleton turned to the sergeant.

'Now, my good man, you may move your cannon into Irishtown and, with my Lord Cromwell's permission, make as much noise as you like.'

Lord Stapleton and Bishop Watkins led the procession from Irishtown amid jeers from within the walls of Kilkenny. They passed the sergeant tackling his cannon for Irishtown. When safely through, the bishop and the lord sat side by side as the townspeople passed. The bishop broke the silence.

'What will history say of this day, will it be seen as a betrayal of God and the King?'

'Who knows?' Lord Stapleton replied. 'But you have given those people passing us by a chance to write it, and their descendants will get a chance to change it.'

Stapleton turned his escort for home. He felt some satisfaction for a job well done. Then his thoughts drifted back to Landers who would have been justified in hanging him, instead left him in the care of his tenants. Why? He knew why. In the hour before they released him, he had found out more about them in that hour than a lifetime of his old ways. His old self would have hung the bishop. Instead, he had treated him with respect. That respect had handed him Irishtown. It was all because of Landers. He was sorry he was dead. He would never get the chance to thank him before he killed him. The portly sergeant led his cavalcade into Irishtown and set up his cannon. His simmering discontent with Lord Stapleton's rise through the ranks forgotten as he dropped his hand, the signal for the cannon to roar. The shot landed within the city of Kilkenny. 'Load,' he ordered, his mind elsewhere. Lord Stapleton had brought a cleric into Irishtown. 'Fire. Load. Fire.' And the townspeople had taken terms. 'Load'.

'I will do the same in Clonmel,' he concluded. 'Fire'.

Cromwell looked across at Lord Stapleton as they sat their horses looking down on Kilkenny. Smoke and dust flew in the air as the sergeant instructed his gunners.

'I can hear it from here,' Lord Stapleton said, almost to himself. 'Despite the cannon, I can hear his voice.'

'Why do you pick on him so much?' Cromwell asked. 'He does his best. Look at him down there, covered in smoke and sulphur.' Lord Stapleton mused.

'He reminds me of someone.'

'Someone you used to know?' Cromwell inquired.

'No, sir. Someone I used to be.' Cromwell was about to question further when the white flag went up over Kilkenny.

'Well, sometimes it works,' Cromwell pointed out as they rode to take possession of Kilkenny. The sergeant came to meet them; the whites of his eyes shone through the grime of his face.

'Well done, sergeant,' Cromwell said. The whites of the sergeant's eyes expanded, and a not-so-white tooth flashed in pleasure.

'I will get a horse and join you,' the sergeant offered.

'I think not,' Lord Stapleton replied. 'Your general appearance would give the impression we were finding it difficult. They might well decide to fight on.' The sergeant looked from Lord Stapleton to Cromwell and swallowed his reply.

'You shall ride beside me when we take Clonmel,' Cromwell offered.

'Clonmel,' Lord Stapleton exclaimed.

'Have you been there?' Cromwell asked.

'No, but I look forward to visiting a grave in that place.'

'A relative?' asked Cromwell.

'No. Just a man called Landers.' The sergeant looked happier as Cromwell and Lord Stapleton trotted off towards the meeting under the white Kilkenny flag.

THE SERGEANT

The sergeant searched the chicken leg for more flesh; there was none. He flung down the bone. It landed at the feet of Lord Stapleton who raised an eyebrow at him. The sergeant hoped he might take offence. The lord remarked 'pig'.

'What did you say?'

'Pig,' the lord repeated. The sergeant was pleased.

'Are you calling me a pig?' he rose to his feet.

'Merely pointing out a ham more suited to your appetite,' Lord Stapleton answered, pushing the chicken bone back towards the sergeant with the toe of his boot. The sergeant sat. Someday, he thought, I will knock that superior smile off his face. He watched the lord who had relapsed into a doze. How could he annoy him to the point of violence? If he could, he would show him what lay under the surface fat; the only time the lord's expression had shown any expression except boredom was when he had mentioned the name 'Landers'. He watched the dozing lord. 'Tomorrow we march on Clonmel,' the sergeant announced. 'I have appointed another gunner to take my place. I will ride beside my Lord Cromwell when we enter Clonmel in triumph over the dead bodies of the mercenaries that held the north gate. This time we will find a use for your cavalry. You will ensure O'Neill will not exit through Irishtown to save them.'

A soft snore came from the lord, who had tilted his chair back for comfort.

'The townspeople think the mercenaries are the spawn of the devil. They say that satin himself leads them – a man called Saunders. The snoring had stopped.

'No, not Saunders,' the sergeant mused. 'Landers'. The chair went over backwards. The sergeant smiled as the Lord picked himself up. 'Do you know him?' the sergeant asked innocently as Lord Stapleton ran out telling his men to mount up; they were bound for Clonmel. The sergeant was pleased now. He could show them he was not just a gunner. He pulled back the flap of the tent and shouted, 'Bring in the priest.'

He approached Clonmel under a white flag, the priest linked between himself and another soldier. The priest bore the marks of a slow learner but, in the end, he had learned the few simple sentences he was now asked to repeat. The booming voice of the sergeant rang out over Clonmel. 'Fr Mulcahy would like to address his flock. Go ahead, Father,' the sergeant prompted. The priest drew a big breath.

'My brethren. I am requested to beseech ye to open the gates of Clonmel to the forces of the English Parliament.'

He needed a while after that to recover his breath as the sergeant nodded approval. 'Fight them,' he roared. 'Send them to hell where they belong.' The sergeant dropped the priest, who sank to his knees, head bowed for the sergeant's sword. As his head rolled down the slope, the sergeant kicked over the still-kneeling body. He walked back up the hill, only to be met by Lord Stapleton, who politely said, 'Nice try, sergeant. You spent hours teaching him a few sentences, and he went and got it wrong. Some people are just slow learners,' Lord Stapleton concluded as he turned his horse and trotted off.

THE HORN

We watched the priest die with honour. They began to parade again. The four horsemen sat on top of the hill as the cavalry rode past in pairs. They took up a position facing the west gate and sat there. This time there would be no help from O'Neill. From behind the cannon came Joshua and his blackclad troop. They took up position on the east gate. Then the regular foot soldiers trooped past, taking up position facing our gate. The horsemen took up position in front of them and led them back behind the cannon. The gunners stood there with torches raised. A shouted command and the torch descended.

'Ceremonious bastards,' said Wexford as we dived for cover. It seemed to last forever, as bits of iron and stone flew overhead. When the cannon went silent, the battlements were no more. A twelve-foot wall and inside gate was all that was between us and the regular army that calmly began to walk downhill, some carrying ladders.

Wexford's men took up their positions on the walls, as did the garrison soldiers at each side of us.

'The marks,' I shouted as I ran for our cannon. My crew were waiting.

'The first mark,' Wexford called. The torch came down. 'Hit,' shouted Wexford from the wall. Urgently, the barrel was dropped and loaded at the same time. 'The second mark,' shouted Wexford. The torch came down. Jesus shouted Wexford. We were on target, describing havoc, but we were not listening, as the barrel came down and loaded. 'Mark,' called Wexford. We fired our third ball. Muskets were firing now as they came in range. The roar of battle filled the air, mixed with the screams of the wounded and dying. Wexford had his men lying flat with muskets resting on rubble that was the remains of the battlements, loaded muskets being exchanged for empty by our men on the ground. As one died or was wounded, another replaced him. They reached our wall and ladders were put up against it. They had got under the arch and were battering the gate. While all this was going on, men stood guard at each door on our street with a stretcher service bringing the wounded to the house in which they lived. Fr Casey was a busy man, caring for the wounded and the dying with my reformed ladies helping. The thought struck me; he would not make bishop by working our street. The cannon on the hill opened up again, and somewhere in the middle of the chaos, I thought I heard a horn blow.

THE PEN

James had watched Cromwell's deployment of the parliamentary forces; it was as he expected. Cromwell had sent the cavalry to the west gate to keep O'Neill in, the puritans east to hold the garrison troops, the regulars to make the breach. Then Joshua's for the extermination.

'It was what he would have done himself,' mused James. Cromwell had no reason to believe there was a threat from behind his lines. That was what James had counted on. Except for the gunners and a camp behind it, the cannon was unguarded. He told his men, 'Remember Drogheda, Wexford and Poulakerry. There is no need to go over our plans again; there will be no quarter given to those we meet. Tonight we sleep in Clonmel.' James' men dismounted before the camp, leaving some to hold the horses. They circled the camp and came in from all sides, knives and swords drawn. They went tent to tent, slaughtering all they met, wounded and attendants alike pleading for mercy, in vain. Then on to the cannon, as the wagons in the camp were tackled up. The gunners never knew what hit them. They were watching the attack on the walls of Clonmel when hit from behind with slashing knives. Then it was Garcia's turn, as his crew expertly lowered the three cannon and fired the hemp. The shot burst into the massed Roundheads trying to scale the walls. The cannons were reloaded. The Roundheads were in a panic as the second round hit them, scattering bodies and stone in all directions. They broke off and ran east and west to escape. James blew the horn. The horses were brought up and mounted, the cannon tackled up to others, and with the wagons from the camp lined up behind, James led them down the hill. He could see the Roundhead cavalry mounting up. The officers had got the Roundheads organised again, and they were heading back towards the north gate. James blew the horn again; the gate stayed shut. Wexford on the wall was first to react. He jumped off, calling for help to lift the oak beam holding the gate. Others ran down the steps to help.

'Stop them!' I heard the garrison commander shout from the wall. 'Don't let them open the gates.' The garrison troops jumped on Wexford and his men, who were outnumbered and shoved back from the gate. Swords were slashing, but Wexford was getting no nearer to the gate.

'Mark,' I shouted. The bugle sounded again. 'Mark,' I roared. This time I got through to Wexford's thick skull. He knew what 'mark' meant; although locked in mortal combat, he looked around. The soldier saw it too; the hemp was already lit. He jumped into the nearest house; Wexford strangely jumped in after him. The cannon roared. The ball hit the gate right in the middle, blowing planks and splinters through the archway, taking with it the Roundhead troops who had sheltered there in a mess of wood and gore. The cannon were first through; crazed horses slipping and sliding over bloody planks as the cannon wheels crushed any life that remained in the bodies underneath. The wagons came next, then James and his mounted men, who were under attack from both sides, dashed through the arch. The garrison leader was now shouting orders; fearing the loss of the town, rained fire on the troops who were massing to storm the breach. James was shouting, 'Back to the houses. Take your places.' Wexford was shouting the same. The doors along the street began to shut. A horse was brought to my cannon, and it was dragged down the street through the end gate. I ran to my house to take up my position. The door was shut; I banged on the door; nothing happened. From outside the walls, I heard singing. The hairs stood up on the back of my neck. Joshua and his hymn-singing murderous hordes were coming. I looked at the arch; framed there was Joshua and behind him a solid mass of his black-clad religious madmen. They stormed through, filling the street, banging on the doors as they passed, but not for long, as the force of the attack pushed them on. Joshua saw me, and he began to list my sins, some of which I had never heard tell of, but he seemed to know what he was talking about. I stood petrified as he ran towards me. Fr Casey shouted from inside the door.

'Hearing Tom's confession, come back later.' My legs unlocked. I ran for the gate, which was swinging shut. I saw a musket pointing at me through the bars.

'Friend, friend,' I shouted. Garcia pushed the musket aside.

'Welcome, friend,' he said as the gate shut behind me. Joshua reached the gate. He tried to stick me through the bars. Wexford brushed me aside; a slash of his sword, taking the sword from Joshua's hand along with some fingers. Joshua extended his hands through the bars. He still wanted to get to me. I jumped back in alarm. Wexford grabbed both wrists. He hung there on the bars. The cannon was brought to the gate. 'Good cover,' said Garcia, shoving the barrel against Joshua's stomach. The street was full now, and the first wave had reached the gate when Garcia brought down the torch. The memory of Joshua flying through the air heavenwards would stay with me forever, as would the memory of the spray of gore that somehow blew back over us.

'I won't do that again,' said Garcia, white teeth smiling through bloody face. In the street there was carnage – legs, arms, heads seemed to hang in the air before dropping in a row where the shot travelled. At each side of the street, the windows opened and muskets and pistols were discharged into the massed soldiers, and closed again. The next cannon was brought up as lines of muskets behind the gate picked off any enemy who were in a position to shoot. The ones in front could see what awaited them and tried to pull back. They could not because officers believing Clonmel had fallen pushed more and more into the street. Garcia was not happy with his line of fire. 'Search the wagons, I want musket shot, something to spread.' I was off on the run. They were trying to climb the gate and being run through with swords. I searched. We were rich. The pay of the Parliament soldiers was there in sacks of coins. I grabbed a few and ran back to Garcia.

'Their pay,' I said; so many expressions passed his face in seconds. 'Oh well, my friend, we will pay them.' I emptied a bag into the cannon. The torch came down. The ball went down the middle as before, killing gruesomely as before, but the coins spread out; a haze of blood rose into the air. The windows opened again and weapons discharged, then shut. They were piling up, falling over their dead, yet they drove in through the arch. I saw the fear of the ones in front when they were being shoved towards the cannon, unable to go right or left. I wondered in that time before the roar of the cannon did they think of Drogheda and Wexford, did they think of the innocents they slaughtered in the churches, now that it was their turn to die? Did they believe they were doing God's work, the God of peace? O'Neill, with the cavalry gone from Irishtown, sent a troop out and, covered by those on the walls, attacked the Roundheads from the side. This had the effect of pushing the Roundheads into the deemed safety of our street. The doomed soldiers in our street tried to take the battlements but were met by the packed garrison soldiers.

Lord Stapleton had watched James Landers ride into Clonmel through the open gate; his effort to intercept him too late. He noticed the mercenaries were no longer on the wall over the entrance. Why? he asked himself. O'Neill interrupted his train of thought as he burst into his cavalry from behind. A horseman shouting 'O'Neill' was bearing down on him. He pulled his pistol and blew him out of the saddle. Another replaced him. He parried a thrust and hacked his attacker to the ground. Why would you leave a gate open and undefended? his mind asked as O'Neill's men were being driven back into Irishtown. Why would James Landers leave a gate open? His mind rephrased the question. The answer popped straight into his head. He wants them to come in. Lord Stapleton drove his horse up the hill for an overview. He could see into the town. What he saw sent a chill up his spine. The burly sergeant was busy pushing Joshua's fanatics through the gate. Inside the entrance, they were being slaughtered. Even as he watched, the cannon roared again; a red haze rose from the packed soldiers as they fell in rows. Lord Stapleton rode downhill shouting, 'Pull back, pull back.' The sergeant was having none of it. This was his day, his victory. He called for his soldiers to join him as he headed for the archway.

Lord Stapleton brought the butt of his pistol down on the sergeant's head and ordered his troops to fall back. He stopped the officers from shoving soldiers through the arch. They fell back in the direction of Carrick. Lord Stapleton expected a counter-attack that never came. The dissent in Clonmel between the factors, which had led to the construction of the pen going unnoticed, saved the ravaged Roundheads from further attacks. Peace came to the street, broken only by the moans from the living buried under the dead. The doors of the houses opened. Our men began to finish the work, pulling the dead and stabbing the living. The garrison soldiers looked on from the walls in silence. We left them to guard the arch and moved to the bank of the river; our street was no place for the living.

THE TERMS

They were back the next day under a white flag to recover their dead. Cart after cart of corpses left the town under the gaze of the four horsemen, who sat and watched the removal. It took all day; the black-clad minsters saying prayers over each cart as they passed. We buried ours, presided over by Fr Casey, who apologised for not opening the door because of Tom's confession. He was oblivious of everything until the cannon fired as he was giving penance. I looked at Tom. 'Did you confess everything?' I asked. Tom's face reddened. 'What penance did he give you?' I asked suspiciously.

'Be a good Christian,' he replied. Tom's face brightened. 'Then I got him to load for me as I fired the pistol out the window.'

'What now?' I asked James.

'Now,' James said, 'now they will come with the white flag again to discuss terms, while he replaces the cannon, and the men he lost.'

'And us?' I asked.

'We wash the street,' James answered. We formed a bucket chain to wash the gore from the street. Outside the town, a tent was erected, just beyond musket range; a white flag fluttering over it. Then a shouted invitation to the mayor to attend the tent under the protection of Lord Cromwell. An audience gathered on the battlements to watch. While on the hill, now minus cannon, a seemingly endless line of troops took up position.

'That should help the mayor make up his mind,' I observed. The mayor emerged from the tent. He turned and said something to someone inside, then walked back to the town.

'Looks like a man troubled,' said James.

The meeting was held in the town hall. Wexford and James were mindful of their experience in the town hall. Garcia and several armed men flanked us while Tom wandered around the adjoining streets. On entering, only the Mayor, O'Neill and the garrison commander were present. We took our seats. The mayor stood up, cleared his throat.

'As ye all know, I have met with the leaders of the army of the Parliament.' He cleared his throat. 'They have offered the following terms. No action will be taken against the townspeople. They will retain all their possessions. The priests will be allowed to leave, unharmed. The garrison will disarm, all arms to be placed outside the walls.' He shifted uneasily. 'The northern troops to be put outside the walls.'

'To be slaughtered,' interrupted O'Neill.

'No. I have his word there will be no slaughter. They want to ensure no further action will be taken against them. This I have agreed to,' he added. 'I cannot watch people starve. The plague is spreading. We must take terms.'

'I accept the terms,' the garrison leader said. 'We put up a stout resistance. His Majesty could not ask for more.' O'Neill regarded him dourly.

'I would ask something of you,' O'Neill said. 'Will you stand with us outside the wall?'

'I am of the town. I am not required to do so,' answered the garrison leader.

'You refuse?' persisted O'Neill.

'Yes,' said the leader.

'Then your fate lies with the town,' answered O'Neill.

'How long have we?' asked James.

'Till dawn,' the mayor said.

'I will consult my men,' O'Neill said.

'And I mine,' added James. We left; I could feel his eyes on me. I turned and caught a triumphant smile, which quickly disappeared, off the garrison leader's face. We walked in silence back to our street. It would be our last day in Clonmel, and the sun was shining. I went to the bank. It was my place of peace, a place where I did not have to think of the dawn and what it might bring. I heard footsteps. I looked around. It was the mayor's wife. She was looking at me strangely.

'I heard you are leaving in the morning,' she began. She saw the question in my eyes. 'She cannot come. He will not leave her side until you are gone.'

'Thanks,' I said, 'for trying.'

'You will find someone else,' she said. 'Have a family. Be happy.' A tear ran down her cheek. 'The mayor,' she said, 'is a good man. He does not know I was married before or that I had a child. He must do his best for the town, but you must stay safe, my son.' She wrapped her arms around me. I stood as stiff as a plank as it came out. A servant girl. A man who wanted a strong son to be a companion to his other son who was not. A servant girl, who agreed only if she were married, but her son would be hers only in her heart. She had kept to her agreement, and was given a dowry which enabled her to live in Clonmel in comfort. There she met the mayor. 'Martha did a good job,' she said, her tear-stained eyes looked into mine for signs of love, forgiveness. There was none; I backed away from her. Now I remembered. The seduction at the dance. The concern when I was wounded. The scorn heaped on me in the orphanage. The hug when she thought I helped. A mother. I stared at her. 'Say something,' she pleaded.

'Don't worry,' I said coldly. 'Your secret is safe with me.' I turned and walked away.

Darkness fell; it suited my mood. The others were in the street having what I suppose was a going away party with music playing. I was asked to play the drums by a laughing Wexford, but I growled at him. One of Garcia's men offered me some rum; I took it gratefully. I wanted more. 'No more,' said the man with the jar. 'James orders.'

'Where did the rum come from?' I asked.

'Skinny,' he said. 'Captain Skinny now, if you don't mind. He has got rich, paid both ways now, food and supplies in, slaves out, paid by the head. He said he would keep a good one for me.' He rubbed his belly and laughed. I was not in the mood. I saw James and grumbled about the shortage of rum. He looked at me sharply.

'What's wrong with you?' he enquired.

'Nothing that rum could not cure,' I answered.

'No rum,' he whispered.

'Don't think the mayor told the whole story.'

'We leave here tonight.'

'That suits me,' I said. 'Quicker, the better.' I was no company for humans, so I went looking for Sleepy. He was on the bank grazing, and showed his pleasure at seeing me by trying to sink his teeth into my arm.

'Is that your horse?' it was Tom who emerged out of the darkness.

'Yes,' I said, but keep away from him.

'Why he is my favourite horse?' said Tom, rubbing Sleepy's ears and the traitor rested his head against Tom's arm.

'Are you leaving with us, Tom?' I asked.

'O'Neill's men asked me that before they left, but I can't leave the others.'

'O'Neill left,' I echoed in disbelief. Tom and I walked back to our street thoughtfully. James and Wexford were preparing to leave.

'Pack your things,' said James. 'We leave within the hour.'

'We can't leave,' I concluded. 'O'Neill is gone.' James stared at me.

'All the more reason to leave,' said Wexford. James was lost in thought.

'He is right,' he concluded. 'We are the northern soldiers now. We cannot defend the town, and if we leave, we have broken the terms. Clonmel will be like Drogheda and Wexford. Tell the men and see that the weapons are outside the walls,' James said. 'I have someone I must say goodbye to.' He walked to the battlements, up the steps and was gone. I said it out loud.

'He thinks Cromwell will put us to the sword.'

'As do I,' said Wexford. 'We must talk to the men.'

Dawn broke and found us tightly packed outside the town wall. There was a drumbeat coming from Carrick; as it grew louder, we could see them, marching in lines of four following four on horseback. Lord Stapleton was one of the four. They passed our position, then the hand went up to halt. The white flag flew in the hand of Lord Stapleton. They rode up to where James sat his horse, with Wexford on one side, I on the other. Behind us were the ones who professed to have nowhere else to go. Garcia was the one to put it in words.

'James, we would follow you to hell.' The four horsemen halted twenty feet from us. The ugly one nodded to the portly sergeant, who produced a piece of parchment.

'This morning, the Parliament, represented by Lord Cromwell, place the town of Clonmel under its protection, having complied with the terms, weapons and northern soldiers put outside its walls.' Cromwell lifted his hand. The sergeant stopped reading.

'So few,' he addressed James.

'The others left,' James said.

'Ah, cowards in every army,' Cromwell lifted his hand; the sergeant resumed reading.

'It only remains that we witness the death of an officer. Signed this day by Lord Cromwell.' He folded the paper and stuck it in front of his tunic. I looked sharply at Wexford; we knew now what the mayor had been withholding.

'Are you O'Neill?' the sergeant asked James.

'No. He left with the others,' said James, who had got smaller in the saddle.

'Then there is no treaty,' said Cromwell.

'You said the death of an officer, there was no mention of O'Neill,' James pointed out. 'As I represent him, it falls on me to take his place.' He would have handed himself up then, but I grabbed his bridle.

Wexford said, 'We leave as we came or not at all.' He favoured the sergeant with the smirk that I found so irritating. Wexford continued

'If he leaves the line he no longer leads. He was a good leader, he tried to keep order where there was none. I am not like that; the men behind me are not like that. We are paid to kill, not to sacrifice one of our own on the altar of your revenge.'

'Truly all here are officers,' said James.

'Then ye shall all die,' the portly sergeant again.

'Not all,' said James. 'Some will get through the breach.' His voice was so certain. The sergeant looked around, their line continued as far as the eye could see. When he looked back, our ranks had parted; the cannon had entered the conversation. Wexford said quietly, 'When they look for your bodies, they will know not which is horse and which is man.' Lord Stapleton pointed the white flag at James.

'Perhaps you may not have noticed. I carry the white flag.'

'I regret to inform your Lordship, the cannon is colour-blind,' James replied.

'If that cannon fires, my treaty with the town is broken. All within those walls will die,' it was Cromwell again. He fixed James with a stare.

'Babies will again fly with swans,' James said. I looked at him, worried. 'I am invited to die in Clonmel again,' James said. 'This time I cannot refuse.' Wexford shot his arm up; the smell of sulphur stung my nostrils. Garcia's hand was descending when I jumped Sleepy in front of the cannon.

'What madness is this?' I shouted, as Garcia's hand froze in place. 'We fight for coins. Who pays us now? No one.' I answered my own question. 'What is this thing about the death of an officer?' I demanded. 'For one coin I will kill the garrison leader.' The horsemen, who had begun to pull away in a desperate attempt to outrun the cannon, were listening. The sergeant asked, 'And if he kills you?' he inquired.

'I am John Landers of Landers' Hall,' I said. 'I am second in command of our army.' I looked defiantly at Wexford, who looked concerned but said nothing. 'Well,' I asked. 'Which is it – coins or cannon?' I reached out my hand. The sergeant moved to shake it, no doubt glad no cannon.

'I think he requires a coin,' said Lord Stapleton dryly as he flipped a coin in my direction. I caught it deftly.

'I will witness the death of an officer,' Cromwell said, a spark of interest lit up his dead eyes. I dismounted and walked to the gate, which swung open to admit us; the four horsemen rode behind me. The people had been listening and knew, whoever died, they were safe, and were in a festive mood. Even those who had shunned me and treated me with contempt began to see virtue and nobility in me. They proclaimed that loudly as I passed. There was something familiar in the kind of things they said. It was only when an old lady said, 'I will pray for your soul,' that I remembered the funerals I had attended as a priest. Others gave me advice, telling me to beware, he was a fine swordsman; advice I could have done without, as the only use I had for the sword was snagging mangolds for the horses. Finally, I stood in front of his door, sword in hand. One of his cronies scampered out. He would know what I was here for, I thought. He sauntered out, looked at me, then ignored me, addressing the horsemen, 'Am I to understand that you accept the death of this, this, scoundrel,' he settled on, 'as the death of an officer, as agreed in our terms?'

'That is so,' said the portly sergeant.

'Then it is done,' he pulled a pistol from behind his back and shot me in the chest. The breath left my lungs. I went over backwards, staring at the sky. Am I dead? I thought. Then, she was there. She flung herself over me, crying and calling my name. He caught her by the hair, turned, flung her into the house, and banged the door shut. I watched as a bird flew overhead. You're not dead, I thought. The breath rushed back into my lungs and I was up, and as he turned I rammed his body into the door, his terrified eyes looked into mine. It was like the first day, as the thin blade dropped from my sleeve into my hand, but this time there was no stopping. Held between us, the weight of my body drove it through him into the door behind. I waited until the panic in his eyes turned to resignation and went blank before I stepped back. He stayed there.

'I have witnessed the death of an officer,' said Cromwell. They wheeled their horses and were gone. I opened the door. His hands swung a grotesque invitation to enter. I held out my hand for hers; she took it as on the first night we walked through the crowd, heads high in silence. The mood of the crowd had changed. Now they cried, 'The greatness of the garrison leader.' They cited his many virtues. Had he not defended Clonmel stoutly? Did he not, in the end, give his life for Clonmel? Would he not still be alive if the town had not hired a gang of cut-throats and brigands to defend it? Numbering amongst them, a man who would kill such a great and noble man for a coin. I was glad they had witnessed the deal with the Roundheads, as I would not like it said I killed him for his woman. The only one who remained consistent was the old lady who repeated, 'I will pray for your soul,' but she said it sadly like she knew it was a waste of time.

THE LEAVING

It only remained to collect those who wished to come with us. Fr Casey was the only priest; the others preferring to take their chances in less sinful company. Tom would not go with us, though trusting his urchin army to our care. I had given him Sleepy, and enough coins to keep him in flour bags for a long time. He filled my head with his plans for the future, until I saw the mayor's wife, my mother, walk up the street.

'I,' she began.

'Yes,' I said curtly. 'It's time to remove the bandages.' I walked behind her to her house. Wordless, she produced a razor and cut into the mass of bandages. Then, catching an end, she unwound the bandages. The ball from the pistol fell on the floor. I picked it up and handed it to her. 'Keep that as a reminder of an ungrateful son who you gave life to twice, my mother.' I embraced her. I had never seen such happiness in a human face. James blew the horn; it was our time to go. With our women and urchins, we were no different from all others on the road in search of safety. The portly sergeant and Lord Stapleton watched us pass. We had not gone far when they came riding after us. The sergeant shouted.

'I have sent word ahead, and no town will let ye in. Lord Cromwell has been called back to England. When he is gone, I will find ye. Wherever ye go, I will find ye.' James ignored the sergeant and addressed Lord Stapleton.

'Will you also pursue us?' Lord Stapleton gazed thoughtfully at James before replying.

'I would not sleep comfortably in my bed while you roam free. I travel from here to confront O'Neill. I would not like to see you by his side.'

'Your sleep will remain untroubled. I will not join with O'Neill,' James replied.

'Then I bid you farewell,' Lordy said. 'The good sergeant, however, may pursue you. I would like him returned unharmed. I have grown quite attached to him.'

Two days later, the sergeant set out in pursuit, killing all unfortunate enough to cross his path. On arriving at the gates of Waterford, the guard assured him that no one answering our description had been allowed in. Indeed, the only large group to pass the gate were misfortunate slaves in chains bound for England under the care of the infamous Captain Skinny.

The deck shuddered under our feet as we cleared the harbour. We stood huddled together with the rain running down our faces as we watched our stricken homeland disappear into the mist.

Printed in Great Britain
by Amazon

50094247R00166